Lock Down Publications and Ca$h Presents

I0658152

THE MURDER QUEENS 8

RESILIENCE

Written By

MICHAEL GALLON

First Edition 2025

Printed in the United States of America

This is a work of fiction. Names, characters, places, and incidents either are products of the author's imagination or are used fictitiously. Any similarity to actual events or locales or persons, living or dead, is entirely coincidental.

Lock Down Publications
P.O. Box 944
Stockbridge, GA 30281
www.lockdownpublications.com

Like our page on Facebook: Lock Down Publications
www.facebook.com/lockdownpublications.ldp

Stay Connected with Us!

Text **LOCKDOWN** to 22828 to stay up-to-date with new releases, sneak peaks, contests and more…

Like our page on Facebook:
Lock Down Publications

Join Lock Down Publications/The New Era Reading Group

Visit our website:
www.lockdownpublications.com

Follow us on Instagram:
Lock Down Publications

Email Us: We want to hear from you!

PROLOGUE

Sometimes in life, one does not like to harp on their past. Good or bad, there's always that one memory that will cause them so much pain, heartache and anxiety that it may take them a lifetime to get over it. This is what I think of every time I think back to that awful night on that somewhat cold morning in Jacksonville, Florida. It was just after Rhynyia and her crew had left the airport.

If only I had known the dangerous risks we took would cost someone their life, I would have never signed up for the path I chose. Now, as I sit here on this bunk the Federal Bureau of Prisons calls a bed, I have to live with the weight of that horrible morning for the rest of my natural life.

Don't get me wrong—it hurts. It hurts a lot to think back on that tragic moment. The only reason I'm even telling this part of the story is because she would have wanted me to.

This is Part 8 of *Murder Queens*: Resilience.

Chapter 1

Two Days Prior…

The high-powered jet of Pierre Santiago hurried down the runway without clearance. Rhynyia felt good about their flight home. She was peeling off her black attire when she yelled, "Alright Miguel, take us home!" Then she walked to the rear of the plane to wipe away the after-effects of the night's escapade.

She was just about to walk past her sister, seated by the window looking like she might cry. After watching my brother drive away with her father's precious product—and her virgin heart—Natasha must've felt what it really meant to be in love.

"Don't worry, Natasha. Everything will be alright, trust me. If there's one thing I know about my Michael, it's that he's never let me down," Rhynyia said, holding out her hand to comfort her.

"It's not Michael I'm worried about, big sis. It's his wild and crazy-ass brother."

They exchanged a smile as the plane ascended into the dark early-morning skies.

Unbeknownst to Rhynyia and her crew, a few local police officers stood outside their patrol cars, staring into the sky at the luxury plane disappearing into the night.

"Damn, there goes our chance for a promotion, Officer Brown!" the short, fat redneck officer barked at his middle-aged Black partner.

"Yep, maybe next time," Officer Brown replied with a smile. He thought to himself, *I'm glad they got away.*

Officer Paul Brown had been on the force for twelve years. In that short time, he'd seen so much brutality against the Black community from his own department that he was actually relieved whoever was on the plane had escaped.

"Yep, another brother got away. Good for him. Lord knows what would've happened if he had dope on that plane," Brown said aloud, heading back to the patrol car.

"What was that, Brown?" Officer Collier asked from the driver's seat.

"Nothing, Boss. Didn't say a thing," he muttered, still smiling as the plane vanished from sight.

Back on board, Rhynyia returned to her seat and leaned her head back, about to doze off when Maria approached.

"Will you need anything else, Princess?"

Rhynyia cracked one eye open, smiled, and said, "No, my dear lady. Please wake me ten minutes before we land."

"Yes, no problem, Princess," Maria said with a smile, then went about her business.

Just as Rhynyia drifted into slumber, Maria ran back to the cabin in a panic.

"Princess, we have a problem!"

Rhynyia opened one eye. "What is it now?"

"It seems the police have a helicopter on our tail."

"A fucking what?" Rhynyia snapped, both eyes open now.

"Miguel says there's a police helicopter behind us."

"Why?"

"I don't know. But they want us to return to Jacksonville International."

"Yeah, fucking right they do. They must've realized who this bird belongs to!" Rhynyia shouted, jumping up. "Move, I have to get to the cockpit!" She shoved Maria aside and rushed forward. Before entering, she turned back. "Was all the cocaine taken off this plane?"

"To the best of my knowledge, Princess."

"We better fucking hope so, or we'll be sitting in a cell for a long time!" Rhynyia barked, yanking open the cockpit door.

The plane had only been in the air twenty minutes when Miguel first spotted the helicopter. At first, he thought it was a news crew, but when air traffic control ordered him to turn back, he knew what time it was.

"Miguel, where are we?" Rhynyia asked, scanning the controls.

"Right now, over a small portion of the Atlantic Ocean," he said, sweat dripping down his face.

"And how many helicopters?"

"Looks like one. But maybe more," he stammered.

"How do we know it's the police?" she pressed, slipping on a headset.

"They've been telling me to turn around since takeoff."

"I see." She sighed.

"What do we do, Princess?" Miguel asked, staring at her from the co-pilot's seat.

"There's no way we can land this bird back at the airport. If they run dogs through here, they might sniff out what we had on board."

"I know. So what do we do?"

Before she could answer, Maria and Natasha rushed in with more bad news.

"Rhynyia, we have a major problem!" Natasha blurted, her face stern.

"What the hell is it now?"

"There's more cocaine on the plane than we thought."

"What? How much?"

"Ten more kilos. Pure, uncut."

"Is it Father's?"

"I can't tell until we land."

"Well, we won't be doing that now, will we?" Rhynyia said, eyes sharp as she turned to Miguel.

"We have to take this plane where no one dares to go."
Miguel's eyes widened in terror. "No, Princess. I won't put us in that kind of danger!"

"Right now, we don't have a choice. Fly this bitch into the Bermuda Triangle."

"No! I won't!" Miguel shouted.

"Then I will! Move out of my goddamn way!" Rhynyia shoved him aside and grabbed the controls. The helicopter tailed them close—until it saw the jet veering toward the Bermuda Triangle. Then it suddenly turned back.

"How's it look back there?" Rhynyia asked.

"They've turned around," Natasha said, peering out the rear window.

"Good. Now I just need to guide this bird past the Triangle's edge."

"How far are we from it?" Natasha asked nervously.

"I can't tell. The controls for that are acting up." Rhynyia frowned. "How long's it been like this?"

"It started as we got close to the Triangle," Miguel said.

"Fuck," Rhynyia muttered.

Suddenly, a bolt of lightning struck the plane.

BOOOOOM!

"What was that?" she shouted.

Miguel's head snapped toward the sound. "We just lost an engine!"

Rhynyia wrestled the wheel, fighting for control. "I—can't—regain—control! Natasha, pull back on your side!"

Natasha grabbed the controls, but they locked. "What the fuck! Is it supposed to do that?"

"No, señorita. I don't understand!" Miguel cried.

Rhynyia looked around at them all and said calmly, "We're going down. Goddammit, we're going down!"

Chapter 2
Praying for Time

By the time those two clown-ass niggas made it back to Belmont Heights it was dark, with not many people hanging around. That actually worked in favor of the two guys from North Carolina—the less people around, the fewer people they'd have to kill.

"So how we gonna play this one, cousin?" Big Breezy asked as they sat parked across from the projects. They didn't know Mo. Money was just one step ahead of them.

"Chill for a minute, partner. Let me rethink my actions before we both end up like Marquis and shit," Lil Breezy said from the driver's seat. His eyelids nearly covered his eyes—the poor bastard had been smoking trees all day. His stomach growled; it was time for his black ass to get something to eat.

"Well, I don't plan on going out like Big Cuz. The way I see it, we run up in this bitch's crib and blast everybody in that bitch," Big Breezy said.

Lil Breezy was the calm one. He tilted his head toward his cousin and asked, "So you know what apartment she lives in, huh?"

Big Breezy lazily turned. "Nah, I thought you already knew that."

"Nigga please—if I knew that, I wouldn't have followed those stupid-ass niggas out to nowhere!" Lil Breezy spat, getting agitated.

"My bad, kid. I just thought you knew, that's all," Big Breezy mumbled, turning back to the window.

"And don't talk to me like I'm some lil-ass kid. Last time I checked, I was born a few years before your smart-mouth ass."

"Well, my nigga, act like it then!" Lil Breezy snarled.

They both spotted a baser walking by the green garbage dumpsters. "Hey, look right there. You think his ass might know?" Big Breezy asked, pointing.

"How am I supposed to know? Hell, that nigga looks like he's tryin' to find something to smoke," Lil Breezy said.

"Don't worry 'bout it. Let me ask him if he knows where we're lookin'," Big Breezy said as he reached for the door. "Hold up—what's her name again?" he asked with his hand on the handle.

"They call her Mo. Money. But I'm not sure folks know her by that name," Lil Breezy said, lighting his blunt. "Don't worry, I got this."

Big Breezy stepped out. Night had settled; most folks were inside their apartments, cooking or getting their nights started.

A few feet away, Big Breezy called out, "Hey partner— excuse me real quick?"

The baser kept walking like he didn't hear. "Now I know this son of a bitch heard me," Big Breezy mumbled, while Lil Breezy sat motionless in the car.

"Yo son—stop for a minute, I need to ask you somethin'!" Big Breezy shouted. The man paused. "Yeah, what you need, my man?"

"I need to know where this chick named Mo. Money lives at."

"I can tell you if you give me a few dollars so I can get something to smoke," the baser said.

"What?" Big Breezy asked, attitude laced in his voice.

"You heard me, young man. Give me a few dollars and I'll tell you. Better yet, I'll take you and your friend straight to her apartment. If that's okay with you?"

"Hold up, let me tell my cousin what's up," Big Breezy said.

"Sure, go 'head. But don't expect me to stand here all day waitin' on you two clowns."

"Watch your mouth, my nigga. I'll be right back." Big Breezy returned to the car explaining everything. Lil Breezy didn't want to take the man up on the offer at first, but after some convincing he decided to follow.

"Okay, so I give you a few dollars and you gon' lead us right to the little bitch?" Lil Breezy asked. The fiend kept his face half-hidden.

"Yep. That's 'bout right. We gonna do this or what? If not, I got an appointment with a nice piece of crack I can't wait to taste," the man said.

"Go ahead, show us the way," Lil Breezy said. The man turned and walked toward the back of the projects.

"So you sure you know where she lives, right?" one of the guys asked, still unsure who the baser was talking to.

"Yeah, I know exactly where she lives. Hell, I was just at her place earlier visitin' her lovely grandmother," the baser said.

"How many people in the house with her?" Lil Breezy asked—he wanted a heads up on how many residents might be inside. Part of him didn't want to kill innocent bystanders. But after thinking about how they did Marquise, he didn't give a fuck who he left behind with a bullet in their head.

In his hand Lil Breezy held a loaded Glock 32, with a trusty .357 tucked behind his back. The baser didn't know what the men wanted with Mo. Money, but he could sense something serious—both dudes didn't look like they were from Orlando.

"So where y'all from, if I may ask?" the baser asked as they turned behind the building.

"We from North Caro—" Lil Breezy started, then kicked the shit out of Big Breezy, who stopped and turned, glaring. "Dumb-ass nigga, what? You jus' gon' tell this motherfucker where we from?" Lil Breezy snarled.

"Ouch!" Big Breezy rubbed his ass. "My bad." He gave Lil Breezy a mean mug. "What was that?" the baser asked, stopping.

"Ahh, we from Jacksonville, Florida," Big Breezy quickly mouthed.

"Oh really. I hear it's some real foul shit up there."

"Like what? You seem like you know a lot about Jacksonville."

"Nah, not really. Just what folks 'round here be sayin'," the man said, then stopped at apartment 112.

"Bout damn time, my nigga. I thought you were leadin' us to some trap," Big Breezy said as he handed the baser a few crumpled dollars.

"Now why would I do that, when Mo. Money's been waitin' on you guys ever since you two dumb-ass country niggas followed them outta here?" the baser smirked.

"What the fuck?" Lil Breezy shouted, pulling his Glock. Big Breezy froze as the few dollar bills blew into the night. That's when Mo. Money threw back her coat and pointed her weapon at the man's head.

"Blam-blam-blam-blam!" Four rounds cracked like a cannon. Big Breezy caught two in the neck; the first bullet hit his main artery, and his reflex made him grab at his throat. He never got a chance to fire—his gun dropped when the second round ripped through his neck. The other two shots were overkill; he was dead before his body hit the ground.

"Oh shit!" Lil Breezy yelled and tried to run, but Mo. Money was quicker.

"Booka-booka!" Two rounds from her Glock 19 hit him under the back of his knee. "Ahhhh, fuck! This bitch shot me in my legggg!" he screamed as he fell face-first into the dirt.

Sand and grass smeared his face as he rolled onto his ass, now staring down the barrel of Mo. Money's gun.

"You niggas would still be alive if y'all left well enough alone," she growled. "But nah—you two country-ass bamas had to bring y'all monkey asses down here to Orlando lookin' for trouble. Now look at your ass."

Lil Breezy raised his hands. "Listen, ma—you guys killed our peeps, so we came for that. Please, if you let me live, I'll get my black ass back in my car and haul. You'll never have to see my face again!"

"Has anyone ever told you that you talk too much?" She pulled the trigger and filled his chest and face with bullets. His small frame jerked violently with each round. When the smoke cleared, Mo. Money had killed two men in pursuit of her and the crew.

"That's for Freddie B and 'nem. Them boys didn't have to die the way they did," she said, then started back to her apartment.

At the door she told her brother, "Help me get these two in their car. Once they're inside, take it to the salvage yard."

"Okay. What about Grams?"

"Don't worry 'bout her—she's over at bingo right now."

"So you don't think anyone is gonna say anything?" he asked.

"Nah, kid. This is Belmont Heights—you know how folks are. They didn't see nothin', nor hear nothin'. Now come on." She gathered the clothes she'd been wearing, pulled her coat back on, and played the part of a baser looking for a rock.

Chapter 3
Jack Up!

I gotta admit—when I got off the phone with Pierre, my feelings toward that man was all jacked up. But what could I do? She was his daughter, and he seemed mighty sure that she and her crew would turn up somewhere. Where, I didn't know. All kinds of mad thoughts invaded my head, but who was I fooling? There was nothing I could do. I didn't have a plane to fly out and search for her, nor the resources to try to find her.

So what did I do? Hell nah—I didn't just plop back down on my bed and go to sleep.

I had the rest of my team to think about. Besides, it was Tuesday night and the girls were slated to be at Hollywood Nites. So I wasn't surprised when somebody knocked at my bedroom door.

"It's open!" I called, making my way around the bed.

"Excuse me, Michael, do you have the list of girls going to Hollywood Nites with us?" she asked.

"Nah—you might wanna call and find out which ones wanna go," I replied, standing in the doorway and trying to hide my face. There was no way I could let it be known Rhynyia and her family might've died after leaving us in Jacksonville. I had to keep that to myself until I heard more.

"Alright, I'll do that. In the meantime, are you alright?" she asked, like she sensed something off.

"Yeah, I'm good. Just noticing how nice your size-nine ass looks in them spandex," I said.

"Whatever, Mike—stop lusting," she shot back, turning to make sure I got a good look. As the door closed, I fell back on my bed, arms outstretched, wondering how the night would go once the Florida Hot Girls and I hit the club.

A few hours later, me and the girls were picking up the rest of the crew. First stop: Belmont Heights.

"Anybody heard from Mo. Money since y'all got back?" I asked from the truck. We'd been sitting out front waiting.

"Nope," Nicole said from the passenger seat. "I wonder what's taking her. She knows how I am about bein' late to the club."

"You want me to go get her?" Nicole asked.

"Yeah—her ass about to get left," I said as she reached for the door. Right then Mo. Money came running out of the building and hopped in. As soon as she climbed in, my nose caught the smell of gunpowder.

"Hold up—what's that smell?" I asked, watching her squeeze in between Mignon and Entyce.

"What?" she said, defensive.

"That smell—like you was at a gun range or somethin'," I said as she settled.

"Yeah, I smell it too," Mignon said. Entyce nodded. "Sure does—like you just finished shootin'."

Mo. Money took a deep breath. "Well, if you all must know…" she started, looking around. "Two niggas somehow tracked me down here from Jacksonville."

"What? How? What makes you think they was from Jacksonville?" I asked, pulling the truck into park. I was not driving anywhere until I knew what was up.

"'Cause, Mike, the one guy I took out was sittin' right beside me in the hospital waiting room," she said, eyes on me and Mignon.

"Wait—you mean some guy from Jacksonville came to your front door?" Mignon asked. Nicole and Entyce perked up.

"Yes, chick. Not one—two."

"Where they at now?" Nicole asked.

"Right about now they should be at the same salvage yard where Mike's brother took his old bodyguard," she answered.

"How many more people we gotta worry about?" Entyce asked, sitting close.

"I dunno, but I'm pretty sure there ain't nobody else," Mo. Money said. "The only way he found me was 'cause he was sittin' next to me in that waiting room. When I got up to use the restroom, he went through my purse and saw my ID with my address."

I took a deep breath, exhaled, and looked every woman in the truck in the eye—Nicole, Mignon, Mo. Money, Entyce, Tameia, and your girl Strawberry.

"Now, did y'all leave anybody alive that might track us down?" I asked.

"Gee, Mike, that's a question we can't answer right now," Mignon said, then added: "When we finished Marquise off, when we got off the elevator in the parking garage, your boy Malik and his DJ friend stepped on."

"Ah hell nah—don't tell me he seen y'all's faces?" I said.

"No—we had surgical masks on, so they couldn't see us on the security footage," Nicole said.

"And the footage?" I asked.

"Don't worry about it, Mike. Officer Nevermind pulled it from the Jacksonville PD," Mignon said. My head snapped around—Officer who?

"Officer Nevermind," she repeated. "I'll explain later. Now let's grab the rest of the girls before they think we left them."

"Say no more," I said as I started the truck. "And cover that smell up with some perfume. We 'bout to pick up nosy-ass Lil Kitty."

"Yeah, about her—what'd you tell her about not goin' to Jacksonville?" Entyce asked as we pulled out.

"I lied," I said. "But know this: tomorrow night you all have a show in Gainesville. One of the boys says there's an up-and-coming rap group in town and they want you ladies for VIP-room entertainment."

"Oh yeah?" they chimed, voices lifting.

"Yup. That should keep a couple of nosy bitches busy," Nicole said, a wide smile spreading across her face.

Chapter 4
Eating Ass!

Marc Dawg was a young thug from down south. He was up in Orlando visiting his sister, Mo. Money. If I had known she told him to dispose of the bodies, I might've checked behind that kid to make sure he did what he was supposed to do with the bodies and the car. As you'll read later, his ass decided to do something totally different.

"So let me ask you this, Mo. Money," I said as I made a left onto Orange Blossom Trail.

"Yeah, Mike—what is it now?"

"Don't get all beside yourself. I'm just trying to cross all my T's and dot all my I's."

"Okay, Mike. I'm waiting." She curled her lips. "Where did you shoot those two guys at?"

"Right outside where I live. Why?" Her attitude was getting the best of me.

"So what about your neighbors? You don't think somebody saw the whole thing?"

"They probably did. But you must not know the rules of the projects." She shot that back at me like a question and an answer.

"No, I don't. Enlighten me." I turned right—we were just down the road from the projects where Lil Kitty lived.

"Look, Mister. People who live in the projects don't see nothin' and they hear nothin'. They mind their business. Besides, I'm pretty sure them niggas killed four dudes out there."

"Word?" Nicole turned to look. "Yeah—this one jackboy named Freddie B. Dude was fresh outta the pen."

"I heard that name before," Nicole said as I slowed. "Real slime-ass nigga. He hung with a crew—Lester Jackson, Poppa, and a kid named Curtis Williams. I guess those guys lured some niggas off from where I lived. One of them must've killed 'em—they never came back. But the dudes I killed came back."

"Goddamn, that's a lot of killing in one day," I said as we pulled into Lil Kitty's lot.

"Not really. Where we from, somebody gets killed every day. Hell, try living over on Mercy Drive."

"I used to live right down the road from Mercy Drive— over in those Sunrise Bay apartments," I said, blowing my horn twice. "Alright, enough. When she gets in, act like nothin' wrong, you hear me?"

"Yes, father," Strawberry spat.

"Alright, Berry—you've been quiet all evening, don't start now."

Lil Kitty jumped in with that same smile. The first thing she said was, "Damn, which one of you hoes been out shootin' at a range or somethin'?"

"Shut the hell up, Lil Kitty!" Nicole snapped, smirking to hide the truth from our nosiest girl.

"What? I'm just sayin'." She looked around at the truck full of Hot Girls.

"Nothing, Lil Kitty. Now where were you and your so-called friends earlier?" I tried to steer this away from Mo. Money's business. I didn't want Lil Kitty nosing around.

"How'd you know I was with friends, Mike?" she asked, caught. I was slick—but she had me for a minute. I checked the rearview and caught Mignon glaring with a wicked smile.

"Let's just say a little bird told me y'all were about to get into some foolishness." Hearing that, Lil Kitty knew I knew more than she wanted to admit. She cleared her throat and said, "Well, if you must know, Punkin called me and wanted a private show for some of his homies. So I brought a few girls up to Jacksonville."

"So, you and your tricks were goin' up to Jacksonville and didn't even tell Mike?" Mignon asked.

"Well, I figured Mike probably wouldn't wanna take us, so me and my crew decided to go make that bread ourselves."

"Oh really—what makes you so sure it was Punkin who called?" Nicole asked.

Lil Kitty wasn't stupid. She knew we were onto her, so she said, "It mightn't have been Punkin himself, but the call came from his phone." She stared at the back of my head. I shook my head and shot her a cold look.

"What? I can make a few dollars without the whole team, can't I?" she said. All eyes glued on her.

"Well, next time you go make bread on your own, make damn sure you're talkin' to the right person before you make a decision that could cost you and others their lives," I told her like she was family.

"What's that supposed to mean, Mike?" she snapped, serious.

"Don't worry, Lil Kitty. I'll explain at the club." The truck went quiet—until we picked up the rest of the crew.

As I pulled away from the last spot, Nicole whispered, "You sure you wanna tell Lil Kitty what went down last weekend?"

"Not really. But I gotta find out who tried to lure her up there. For all I know, they might know more than we think."

"You right, Mike. Don't worry—I got this."

I hit I-4, heading to Tampa.

Meanwhile, up in Duval County, Trigger was pissed. He'd booked a hotel room for his girls and they hadn't shown. Every call to Lil Kitty went straight to voicemail.

"Damn—this Lil bitch done stood my ass the fuck up!" he shouted, tossing his phone. His partner Cheese walked in with blunts and smoke thick in the air, face blank as hell.

"Yo, where them hoes at? Thought they'd be here by now," Cheese said, puffing.

"Yeah, ugly-ass nigga. I thought that too. But I think them hoes set us up," Trigger spat.

"Set us up? I bought all this weed and we ain't got one bitch to smoke with and then fuck the shit out of," Cheese complained, upset.

"Nigga chill. If anything, I lost the most," Trigger said, hatred in his voice.

"How?" Cheese asked, collapsing into a chair.

"Damn, you forgot why I had those hoes come up in the first place?" Trigger reached for the blunt.

"Oh yeah, I forgot," Cheese said, handing it over.

"Like I said from jump, I think Lil Kitty might know what happened to our boy Punkin," Trigger said, pulling on the blunt and blowing out thick smoke.

Chapter 5
Ass Eating Bandit

Eleven-thirty, the girls and I walked inside the club while patrons were still drifting in. The spot wasn't packed yet, but we knew it would be in a few minutes. Why wouldn't it be? I was there with at least twelve bad-ass females, while my boy Richard had another ten with his high ass.

We sat at the bar, sipping drinks and talking while Mignon took control of both sets of ladies. We had only been seated a few minutes when Ms. Hot-ass Lil Kitty strutted up with half an outfit covering her petite body. Her face held a bright smile, and her eye looked healed up real nice as she cleared her throat.

"Excuse me, Mike?"

"What is it now, Lil Kitty?" I replied, half-turning on the barstool.

"When am I going to be a manager in this damn group of yours?"

I had to look at her little ass good. Once my eyes locked on her and that outfit, I threw a devilish smile on my face.

"When you make up your mind and become my special little lady."

She kept smiling, quick to interject.

"Whatever, Mike. Mignon ain't your special little lady, and she's the manager."

"You do have a point there," I said. "Tell you what—once you stop flaunting that fine ass body around me and these other niggas… especially that tight little Kitty Kat of yours—" I pointed between her legs.

22

She blushed hard, still smiling at me and Richard.

"And what else?"

"Well, once you let me hit that thing the way I want to, I'll let you be the manager."

"Whatever, Mike. You know this pussy is good, and the ass is even better. Just ask your cousin Stubby here." She pointed straight at Richard.

Richard spit out whatever he was drinking. I snapped my head his way while Lil Kitty darted off, laughing loud as hell.

"What? Lil Kitty, get your ass back here! What you mean ask Richard?"

I jumped up, but she kept running, giggling to herself. I turned back to Richard, smirking while he was still choking. I slapped his back a few times till he stopped. His eyes were watery, saliva dripping down his mouth. He wiped it off and avoided my stare.

I leaned over, cracking up. "Hey Rich, what the hell was she talking about? And why she call you Stubby?"

Embarrassment was all over his face. "Man, she tripping. I don't know what she's talking about."

"Okay, Richard. Don't let me find out, playa."

"Find out what, cuz?" He tried to sit straighter, composure shaky.

"That you out here eating ass, nigga. That's what!" I kept a serious look but hid my grin.

He tried to act innocent. "I don't know what she's talking about, but she need to stop that shit."

"Stop what, Rich? If you ate her ass, you ate her ass. That's it."

"Man, please. Why would I eat her lil narrow ass?" He took a swig of his drink.

"Hell if I know. We all do strange shit for a piece of ass, you know?"

"I know that's right." He laughed a little, then leaned closer. "So Mike, let me ask you something."

"Go ahead, ask away."

"You ever hit that?"

"Who, Lil Kitty?"

"Yeah." He tried whispering like we weren't in the middle of a club.

"Come closer," I told him.

"Why?"

"So I can tell you what you want to know since you whispering loud as hell in the club."

He laughed. "Oh, my bad, cousin."

"Okay, does it snow in Alaska?" I asked.

"I guess. I ain't never been there."

"Well, in that case, yes, I hit that."

"Damn, cuz. How was it?"

"Whoa, Rich. Sound like you want a piece of Lil Kitty yourself."

"Nah, not really. Just curious how good it is."

"Well, let me tell you—she got the tightest pussy in this group. Real tight, real good. Makes you want to slap your mama for not telling you about a female like her."

His beady eyes got wide. "What?"

"Yeah, it's that damn good."

"Damn, Mike. I bet you done fucked half the females in this group."

"Nah, not yet."

Right then Chyna drifted out the dressing room looking like an angel. I was smitten by her sheer beauty.

"Mike, all the ladies are dressed. Where you want our bags?"

"Bring them out here, we'll put them in the trucks."

"Thanks." She walked off, hips swaying side to side.

"Cuz, please tell me you beat the brakes off that one?" Rich said, eyes glued.

"Not yet."

"Why?"

"She harder to crack. Plus, she got a man she stays loyal to."

"Okay, I see why," he said as the girls started bringing out their bags.

I stood and addressed them. "Everybody got a Crown Royal bag for your money?"

"Yes, Mike," they answered, all except Tameia, who seemed distant.

"Cool. You know the club rules. If you don't, ask someone who's been around longer. Oh, and tomorrow night we got a show in Gainesville."

"Who with?" Sugar Bear shouted.

"My man says a rap duo is performing. He wants the Hot Girls to entertain."

"What's the group's name?" Peekachu asked.

"The Ying Yang Twins."

"Oh snap!" Lil Kitty hollered. "I heard of them—they climbing the charts with bangers!"

I smiled wide. "Alright, you heard her. Now go get your money. And as soon as you got your tip-out fee, bring me my muthafuckin' cut! First round of drinks on me."

The girls crowded the bar. I moved away, mind drifting. Tomorrow night's show was on my plate, but what troubled me more was not knowing if Rhynyia and her crew had been rescued yet…

Chapter 6
I Want You

Female after female started ordering drinks, while the non-drinkers checked themselves in the full-length mirrors, making sure they looked flawless for the night. Once they had their drinks, they called back, "Thanks for the drinks, daddy!"

"Shut the hell up!" I shouted as they walked away. Still, my mind wasn't on them—it was on Rhynyia and that hot-ass Lil Kitty.

Richard sat there, staring at me, shocked. "Hey Mike, how much are all those drinks gonna cost you?"

"Not a damn thing. The club lets us drink free since I brought them from Orlando."

He looked around, then asked, "Does that mean me too?"

"Yes, Richard, you're with us, right?"

"I guess," he replied, skeptical.

"You are, so no reason to doubt. Go ahead."

He turned to the bartender. "Rum and Coke, please."

"Coming right up, sir," she said.

Richard leaned back, smirking. "Boy, you're a sneaky-ass nigga."

"Nah, who, me?" I smiled, glancing at the guys foaming over my crew. I had some serious stallions with me that night—JK, Mignon, Nicole, Tameia (still distant), Mo. Money, Entyce, Strawberry, Brittany, Charlie B, Tiger, Monique, Candy, Chazz, Peekachu, Sugar Bear, and Eight Ball, a thick hood chick from Palaka, Florida, named for her freaky skills.

The ladies blew me kisses, some kissed my cheek, then hit the dance floor or mingled with whoever wanted them.

"We 'bout to shut this fucka down, Mike!" Mercedes shouted, hyped up as ever.

"Alright, Mercedes, do that, sweet heart," I yelled back.

Mignon was the last to pass, and I grabbed her arm. "Excuse me, Ms. Lady."

Her look said, *let go.* I did. Her lips parted. "Yes, Michael?"

"Keep an eye on Chyna for me."

"Why? What has she done now?"

"She still feels some type of way, knows I'm a little irritated about that stunt with Innocence."

"Whatever happened with Innocence?"

"I have no idea."

"She never called after you sent her back?"

"Nah, not once. She probably feels some type of way since Rhynyia and I sent her home."

"I see. So Chyna might still be in contact with her?"

"I don't know. I need eyes on her conniving ass at all times."

Mignon snapped me out of my trance. "Anything else I need to do tonight?"

I hesitated, then said, "If I told you what I really needed, you'd just laugh and walk away."

"Whatever, Mike. For real, what is it?"

"You, Mignon. It's you I want."

She pulled me closer, a serious unit on her gorgeous face. "That's one reason I'm leaving the group, Michael."

"Why? Because I want you?"

"Have you thought it might be me who wants you?" She kissed me, sashayed away, making sure I saw that red-hot ass of hers.

"Damn!" I whispered, stunned. Watching her disappear into the crowd, daydreams about her flooded my mind. I stood there, mouth open, peppermint scent on my breath, heart racing.

Mignon was one of the finest females in my group. Crossing that line would cause more problems than I could handle. I never thought she'd be interested, but now I understood why she was leaving.

Ten minutes passed in awe until DJ Teddy Bear cranked up *Still Fly* by Big Tymers. I backed down, sitting beside Richard, while haters shot us envious looks. My top-notch females hit the stage, gyrating on poles, sending the crowd wild.

"Hey Mike, did I just see what I think I saw?" Richard asked, mouth agape.

"What did you see? My head's still spinning," I replied.

Teddy Bear hyped the club over the mic. "Ladies and gentlemen, live and in full effect! The Florida Hot Girls, with Orlando Mike! Show some love for the eight wonders of the world!"

"Throw some money at Mignon and Nicole on stage. Left of them, Tameia. Right by her, Charlie B!"

Richard nudged me. "So, you're not answering my question?"

"My bad, cousin. I'm still in La-La land."

"If her bad ass kissed me, I'd already be eating out her ass," he said.

"So that's what Lil Kitty meant?"

He spit his drink, bolted for the men's room. I caught Lil Kitty out of the corner of my eye. I still had to talk to her, but Mignon's performance had me entranced. I leaned closer, about to approach the stage, when a tug on my arm stopped me. The female of the hour…

Chapter 7
Forever!

My eyes locked on hers. "Yes, Lil Kitty, what is it now?"

She looked at me with those cute little eyes, then sucked her teeth, hands on her hips. "I thought you had something to talk to me about."

"I do… but not now."

"If not now, when, Mike?" She made sure I didn't walk off.

"Let me check something out, then I'll find you," I told her as I headed to the stage. I had to witness poetry in motion—Mignon was that poetry, and I needed every word.

On stage, she danced like her body was speaking directly to me. "Damn, you fine!" I whispered under my breath. She must have read my mind, because I could swear she looked right at me and said, *I want you and that dick all up inside me, right now!* My head spun side to side, then back to her.

"You serious?" I asked. She just nodded, yes.

I won't lie—I was in love with a few girls in the group, but Mignon had me completely. Ever since I first spotted her at Apollo South, I had wanted her. But with Rhynyia by my side, I could never choose her. Now, with Mignon and Rhynyia close, crossing that line was risky… yet I wanted the biggest one of them all.

Meanwhile, Richard emerged from the men's room, eyes wide. The first thing he saw was the girl whose booty he'd sampled. He shouted, "Lil Kitty, bring that ass here!"

She was busy on her phone, raised a finger. "Hold on!"

After a quick call, she muttered to the line, "Like I said, shorty, what happened with you and your girls?"

"My car got a flat on the way to Duval, but we're good," she explained. "I wanted to be there to chill with my lil boo thang."

"I know right, he feels the same way."

"Where's his fine ass? Why isn't he on the phone?"

Trigger faked it fast. "Hold on, he's in the bathroom," he said, covering the receiver. "Yo Punkin, it's your girl Lil Kitty!"

She smiled. "That's right, I'm your girl," she mumbled.

A voice yelled from the bathroom: "I'm using it right now!"

"Did you hear him?"

"Yeah... just have him call me later," she said, suspicious. *Something's off.*

Trigger sensed it too. "I think the lil bitch is on to us."

"Why?" Cheese asked, lighting a cigar.

"Your ass didn't sound like our partner, Punkin."

"My bad, but how's a dead man supposed to sound?"

Trigger muttered, "Watch your mouth," and walked to the balcony, head down, thinking about avenging his homie. Cheese followed with the blunt.

"Don't worry bruh. They come up here every weekend anyway. If not, let 'em come to us."

"Yeah, but they won't if they have another show."

"I say we go to Orlando and find them hoes," Trigger said.

"Word," Cheese replied. "I've got two cold-ass niggas from North Carolina ready to get their hands dirty."

"Let me call them," Trigger said—unaware they were just as dead as Punkin.

Back at the club, Nicole passed Lil Kitty after she and Mignon finished their set. "What's wrong, Lil Kitty?"

"I just got off the phone with a guy with my boo thang, Punkin. He says Punkin wants me in Duval..."

"Okay, so what's wrong?"

"Punkin never comes to the phone. Something's up. I almost went up there today," she said as Mo. Money walked up.

"Something about Punkin?" Nicole asked.

"If you knew like I do, I'd erase that nigga's number," Mo. Money said.

Nicole looked at her sideways. "Are you serious?"

"Yes! Now think fast—she's right behind you," Mo. Money warned.

Richard, watching at the bar, muttered, "These hoes and Mike have more going on than we know."

"What was that, Rich?" I asked, sitting beside him.

"Nothing, just tripping on your girls," he said, pointing at the intense conversation.

Mignon leaned to my right shoulder and whispered, "I can't wait to get back home," smiling before sashaying into the ladies' room. I sat there, rock hard, mind spinning.

A few hours later, after dropping every female off, I was about to close my eyes when a light tap at my bedroom door startled me.

"Now who the hell is this?" I mumbled as I opened the door.

To my surprise, it was Mignon, playing Anquette's *Forever...*

Chapter 8
I Will Always Be There For You!

I was just as shocked as anyone else when she stood there half-naked in a red negligee. The garment left nothing to the imagination, her red thongs teasing perfection.

"Mignon, what's this?" I asked.

She placed a finger over my lips. "Shhh, less talking. Are you going to let me in or what?"

"Hell yeah, please do."

As she walked past me, her perfume engulfed me—it wasn't just fragrance; it was angelic. Once the door closed, she sat on the bed and peeled open her negligee, revealing her perfect C-cups.

"Do you want to see how they taste?" she whispered.

"Hell yeah," I said, sliding between her legs. My lips hungrily found her breasts, sucking like a newborn, while below, my dick throbbed uncontrollably.

"Nigga, stop playing. Let me show this chick how we get down!" Johnboy shouted.

"Hold on, I need these titties first," I said with a mouthful.

She moaned. "Umh... ahhh... what?"

"Nothing, Mignon... just soft as hell," I muttered.

She grinned, "If you think those are soft, wait until you taste her," then eased back, spreading her legs.

"Oh shit!" I exclaimed at her shaven pussy, heart pounding like an African drum.

"Come taste my kitten," she smirked seductively. I dove in, slurping like a kid on his first ice cream cone.

"Damn, Mike, you eating this pussy like a mango," she moaned.

"Wait until I put all ten and a half inches inside your tight pussy," I teased.

"I can't wait," she replied, sliding her finger along her lips.

Dropping my boxers, I revealed my rock-hard manhood.

"Oh my… all that for me?"

"Damn skippy," I said, easing back onto the bed.

"Wait… first let me ride it," she commanded.

"Go ahead, young lady," I said. She climbed atop me, hands behind my shoulders, pussy aligning perfectly. Sliding down my shaft, she moaned, "Um, oh shiiiitt… got damn, feels so deep."

"If I'm not there yet, I will be," I said.

"Shut up, Mike, make love to me," she demanded.

"As serious as a heart attack," I replied, wrapping her in my arms and laying her down. I went for broke, thrusting into her tight, gripping pussy.

"That's because I don't fuck around. You're the first person to hit this since joining the group," she said.

"Never seen you leave the club with anyone," I noted.

"Exactly. Now stop talking and make love to me," she said.

I obeyed. Her wetness allowed me to slide freely, each stroke driving us both wild.

"I'm not stopping until the war is over," I growled.

"Okay, Prince," she whispered, referencing my favorite hit.

Then, Anquette's *I Will Always Be There For You* played. Her voice, soft and tender, filled the room:

"I never met a person quite like you. Someone who makes me feel loved. I want to be the one that you're thinking of… Forever, and ever. I will always be there for you. I promise."

I was so lost in her, I didn't notice the tears rolling down her cheeks.

"Mignon… are you alright?" I asked.

"Yes, Michael. No man has ever made love to me like you," she whispered.

We continued to make love, not realizing that someone else was inside the house watching us the entire time.

"Michael, always know that just like the song says, 'I will always be there for you'."

"And I will be there for you too, Mignon," I told her as I continued going in and out, out and in. I was even moving my hips in a circular motion, making sure I hit every wall, every corner of her fitting pussy. I was bent on making her ass fall in love with me and my manhood.

Thirty minutes later is when I placed her legs up over my shoulder and started long-dicking her fine ass…

Chapter 9
Wads of Hundreds!

It was bright and early on a Wednesday morning. Firstborn and his two-man goon squad were at the Tallahassee airport, dressed to impress as they headed inside to board their flight to Puerto Rico. Pierre didn't feel comfortable sending another one of his planes, so he had Firstborn book a flight and promised to reimburse him once they arrived in San Juan. Pierre's men would pick them up there.

Firstborn was all smiles as he stepped up to the front counter. "We have first-class seats for the flight that leaves at noon for Puerto Rico."

The lovely assistant shot him a shy smile. "Sure, sir, let me check. And what name are the seats reserved under?"

"They should be under James Vallentino Jr., ma'am."

"That was James Vallentino Jr., right?" she asked, still smiling.

"Yes ma'am, three first-class tickets under my name."

His deep baritone seemed to rattle the elegant receptionist as she searched her computer. Blushing, she looked back up at him. "Oh, I'm sorry, sir. Here's your reservation. Yes, I see three seats reserved for you and your associates. That'll be fifteen hundred dollars, sir."

"That's correct. First class, right?"

"Yes, sir. And how will you be paying? Cash or credit card?"

Firstborn smirked, pulled out a wad of hundreds tightly wrapped with a rubber band. A few people in line started whispering.

"They gotta be some type of drug dealers, carrying money like that," one nosy white man muttered to his wife, who turned her nose up.

Twan looked straight at their eighteen-year-old daughter, grabbed his crotch. The young beauty smiled back when she noticed the huge bulge in his tailored suit. She was so caught up she barely heard him say,

"Slide me those digits, sweetheart, and I promise I'll make you feel like a damn princess."

Her cheeks flushed red as she scribbled her number on a torn piece of her boarding pass, sneaking it over without her parents noticing.

"Thank you, Mr. Vallentino. Here you are, three first-class tickets. Please enjoy your flight," the attendant said.

Firstborn slid her his number and a napkin-wrapped roll of bills. "Call me when you get off. Here's a little something to buy yourself something nice."

She quickly pocketed his number and the two grand without looking up, then moved to the next customer, sneaking him a wink.

"Damn, Smooth, boy, you're just as smooth as your gotdamn brother!" Twan laughed as they headed toward the gate.

Firstborn chuckled, and the three hurried down the corridor, unaware of what lay ahead.

He had the whole day planned. They'd land in San Juan around two, meet Pierre at three-thirty, pay him, re-up, and catch a private plane back to Tallahassee loaded with yayo before anyone noticed they were gone. No time for Natasha, and he didn't even know if she or Rhynyia had been found or rescued. Still, all he cared about was Mr. Santiago's drugs.

The trio buckled up as the pilot's voice came over the intercom. "May I have your attention, please? This is your pilot, Captain Gabriel Gaskins. Thank you for flying Mid Eastern Airlines. The weather in San Juan is ninety-eight degrees with a chance of afternoon showers. We'll be taking off once the pattern is cleared, so sit back and enjoy your flight."

"Damn, the pilot sounds like a brother!" Fabian said, turning to Firstborn, who was staring out the window, whispering a prayer.

Father, I know you don't approve of this life, but if we make it back safe, I promise I'll quit. That is, once I become a self-made millionaire.

Firstborn finished praying and looked back at Fabian. "Yeah, he did."

"Hell yeah, like a college-educated brother," Fabian replied. "By the way, did you finalize the rental?"

"Yes, sir. Got you a Cadillac truck, and Twan and I got something special too."

"Cool. I'm about to lay back and get some sleep. Wake me when we land." Firstborn slid his Gucci shades on and leaned back.

"So I guess that leaves you and me, huh, Twan?" Fabian asked.

"Nah, my brother. You see that lil' white thing back there to the left?"

Fabian glanced over. "Who, the one smiling at me?"

"That'd be her. But she ain't smiling at you, she's smiling at me."

"What? How you so sure about that?" Fabian asked.

"Because I told her as soon as the plane takes off, head to the bathroom and I'd meet her inside to show her something she never seen before."

"Stop lying. That girl ain't thinkin' about your black ass."

"Okay. Sit back and watch what happens as soon as this muthafucka takes off."

Chapter 10
The Call!

Five hours earlier, at the Santiago Estate, Pierre had been asleep a few hours when the phone rang on his private line. He rolled over, answered. "Hello."

The voice on the other end spoke so fast, in broken Spanish, that Pierre cut him off. "Hold on. Calm down. Let's try this again."

"Sí, Señor Pierre," the frantic caller said, then slowed down. Whatever he said made Pierre slide out of bed.

"Where?" Pierre asked.

"Somewhere near a small island off South Carolina."

"I see. Were my people found safe and alive?" Pierre asked, showing the first sign of concern since hearing about the accident.

"We don't know yet, sir."

"I understand. Well, have my men continue the search."

"Sí, Señor. But I must tell you one thing." His voice trembled. "The plane seems to have gone down over shark-infested waters."

Pierre snapped. "Listen here, Hector! I don't give a damn where it crashed. One thing I know about Rhynyia—she got resilience in her blood. That means her and her family are still alive, no matter if they crashed in shark waters! Do you understand me?"

"Sí, Señor."

"Okay. Now find my gotdamn family!" Pierre barked, slamming the phone down before Hector could respond.

"Is everything okay, Pierre?" his wife asked, sitting up in bed.

He didn't want to tell her what Hector said. "They think they found parts of my plane."

Her eyes widened. "So that means they found our family?"

He lowered his head. "No, my dear. Hector says they don't have any info on them yet."

She looked crushed, so he added, "But don't worry. Like I keep saying—Rhynyia was born with resilience. That same resilience will bring her and the rest of them back home to us."

Tears filled her eyes. "How sure are you of this?"

"Because it's in my veins too," he said with pride.

"Well, let's pray they're safe and returned to us," she whispered.

"Right now, me and the man upstairs ain't seeing eye to eye with how I've been living," he muttered, sliding back into bed.

"And what's that supposed to mean?" she pressed.

"Not right now. I'll explain later," he said, closing his eyes. He needed rest for the long day ahead.

Back at the Vallentino Estate, Mignon and I had fallen asleep in each other's arms. Her head lay on my chest as she snored softly. Right before she drifted off, she looked up.

"You know my lil' coochie kat gonna be sore as fuck in the morning?"

I grinned. "So you want me to slide inside that fine ass of yours too, make both holes mad at me and my long dick?"

"Nigga, you got Mignon fucked up if you think I'ma let you put that dick in my tight ass hole."

"My bad, lil' mama. Just trying to look out for both your holes, that's all."

"Whatever, Mike. Get some sleep. We got a long day ahead," she said with a smile.

"You right, Mignon, we do." She laid her head back down on my chest. Neither of us realized the chaos that would come if our secret was ever exposed. Neither of us knew someone was outside my door, filming everything. If we had … maybe things wouldn't have ended with somebody losing their life over one mistake.

***

That same morning, Marc Dawg was rolling out of bed. He'd been laid up with two strippers from a club off Orange Blossom Trail.

"Damn, what time is it?" he asked, sitting on the edge of the bed, mind scattered.

"I don't know, but I know one thing," the slim stripper said, standing up with nothing but a sheet around her.

"What's that?" he asked, reaching for his pants.

"Me and my homegirl need that money you owe us for our services." She plopped her thin ass on the toilet seat, pissing loud.

"Oh yeah, don't worry. I'ma grab it from the car right now," he told her, pulling his pants up. He smirked at the light-skinned one still asleep.

"Damn, lil' mama, you got some nice ass pussy," he muttered.

The skinny one walked out the bathroom without washing her hands. "While you're out, grab me and my girl some breakfast too!"

"Damn, lil' mama, you nasty as hell not washing your hands," he said, staring.

She smacked her lips. "Don't worry 'bout me. Just get that bread and bring us something to eat, my nigga!" She slid back in bed next to the one he really wanted.

"Whatever. Wait right here. I'll be right back." He laced up his Jordans.

"Hurry up, my nigga!" she called, pulling the covers over her head.

"Yeah, right, trick," he thought, walking out. He hopped in his Bonneville, started it up, smirking. "Good luck with breakfast and that bread. Only thing y'all getting is dick." He laughed as he pulled out the lot—never realizing two dead bodies were still in the trunk.

Five hundred miles away, wreckage from Pierre Santiago's private jet washed up on a small island off South Carolina. The man who found it immediately called the Coast Guard.

They told him they were already aware of the crash. To their knowledge, there were no survivors from the aircraft carrying Pierre Santiago's immediate family—one of the most feared cartel bosses alive.

Chapter 11
Missing!

Cheese had been trying to call Lil Breezy all morning, but all he kept getting was the kid's voicemail. After crashing out, he figured he'd try again later. He wouldn't need their services until the end of the week anyway—just wanted to touch base, put the jit up on game.

Cheese was rolling over in the hotel bed when Trigger walked in.

"Yo son, it's almost check-out time. You paying for another night or what?"

"Nah, kid. I'm 'bout to get up right now," Cheese replied, yawning as he sat up. "What time is it anyway?"

Trigger glanced at his watch. "Like I just said, my nigga—it's check-out time. Now, did you get in touch with them fools from North Carolina?"

Ever since bodies had been dropping, Trigger felt they needed more hittas on point.

Cheese rubbed his eyes. "Man, shit is crazy. I been calling Lil Breezy all morning. He ain't picking up."

Trigger stared. "You don't think something bad happened to them fools, do you?" His face went dull.

"I don't have a clue, but let me try this nigga one more time," Cheese muttered, reaching for his phone on the nightstand. He dialed Lil Breezy's number. Instead of ringing and going to voicemail like earlier, it went straight there.

"That's odd," Cheese said, shutting the phone.

"What's that?" Trigger asked, brows furrowed.

42

"This morning his shit rang five times before it hit voicemail. Now it's going straight there."

Trigger's greasy face fell. "When you talk to him last?"

"Just the other day, right after they found out about Marquise."

"Which Marquise? The one who owned the rib joint on Beaver Street?" Trigger asked, pulling the curtain open to let sunlight flood the dim room.

"Yep, that Marquise," Cheese said, squinting against the light.

"Damn. You don't think them brothers met their maker, do you?" Trigger shook his head.

Cheese sighed. "All I know is, last time we talked he said him and his cousin were headed to Orlando."

"For what?"

"Something about some lil' stripper bitch named Mo. Money."

"Mo. Money," Trigger whispered.

"What—you know her?"

"I know I heard that name before," Trigger said, pulling out his phone.

"Oh yeah? Where?"

"If I'm not mistaken, she dances with the same clique as that one female, Lil Kitty."

"You sure?" Cheese asked, easing out of bed.

"I don't know, but I'm 'bout to text this lil' trick right now," Trigger said, typing fast.

Hey boo, it's me. The reason I'm texting is my girl in the bathroom and I don't need her catching me on the phone. Is there a chick in your group named Mo. Money?

He set the phone down on the dresser. "Now let's see if this lil' bitch hits me back."

"So if she is in their group, what we gonna do then?" Cheese asked.

"We travel down to Orlando and do these hoes. That's what we do," Trigger said, not realizing death was already circling. Death had a name, too—*The Murder Queens.*

***

A few minutes past noon, Lil Kitty got the text from Punkin's phone. A wide grin spread across her face. At first, she thought not to respond—she still wasn't sure if it was really Punkin. But when Mo. Money's name popped up, she couldn't help herself. She was still heated about the ass-whooping Mo. Money had put on her.

Yeah boo, she dance with us. Now why you asking about that hoe? You tryna fuck her too? she texted back.

Cheese reacted quick, thumbs moving. *Nah, my partner who been calling you wants her, that's all.*

***

Meanwhile, up in the sky… The plane carrying my brother was climbing into the clouds when the pilot came over the intercom.

"I'm about to turn off the fasten-seatbelt sign so y'all can walk freely about the flight. We'll be cruising at thirty-five thousand feet. Please enjoy your flight, and once again, thanks for flying Mid Eastern Airlines."

Ping-ping!

The light blinked on. Passengers unbuckled.

Fabian threw his arm across Twan's chest. "Hold on. Where the hell you going?"

"You see that lil' white girl I told you about?" Twan asked, eyes locked on his brother.

"Yeah."

"Okay then. Pardon me, big brother." He shoved Fabian's arm down.

"Hold up. Where she go?" Fabian pressed.

"Like I said—her lil' hot ass probably in that bathroom waiting on me to show her something she ain't never seen before. Now move your leg so I can put this dick on her ass!"

Fabian glared. "Man, fuck you."

"Nah, that's what I'm about to go do," Twan laughed. "While your black ass stays out here with sleepyhead." He pointed at Firstborn, who leaned against the window.

"I heard that," Firstborn mumbled.

"Oh, my bad, Smooth. Thought you was asleep."

"Not quite yet, Twan. Now go handle your business before I handle it for you."

"Damn, Smooth, that's how you feel?" Twan smirked.

"Yes sir. A woman should never be kept waiting. Especially if she 'bout to get the fucking of her young life." Firstborn lifted his shades, eyes serious.

"You don't gotta tell me twice. I'll be back in a few minutes. Don't wait up." Twan grinned, sliding down the aisle.

"Do you, lil' nigga," Smooth said, looking at Fabian with a smile before leaning back.

For Firstborn, it was his first real flight—besides that trip to Puerto Rico with me. Nerves should've been there, but the hunger for millions made it all just part of the game.

Chapter 12
Right Cheek!

Twan casually walked up to the bathroom door, knocked lightly, and waited for her voice.

"Someone is in here."

"It's me," he voiced as the door slowly slid open, just far enough for the very attractive young lady to see who was knocking. An innocent but shy smile immediately appeared on her face as she saw her young beau standing there.

"What took you so long?" she quickly asked as she reached up and pulled him into the bathroom.

"My bad, I had to get permission before I left my seat."

"Are you serious?" the young eager lady asked as she reached for his belt.

"Hell yeah!" he told her, noticing how quick she was to go for the dick. "You sure don't waste no time, do you?" he asked as she ripped his belt from his waist.

She looked him directly in his eyes. "It's not that—it's just when someone promises me something, I really want it."

His pants hit the floor, revealing his sport boxer briefs.

"Alright now, when you see what you're about to wake up, you're gonna have to deal with it," Twan uttered as he felt his emotions start to rise.

"No problem, big daddy. Let me worry about that. Besides, I'm a big girl," she muttered as their lips locked in a passionate kiss. Seconds later, he pulled his lips back, gazing at the young female with sweat beads forming on his forehead.

"Damn, lil ma, slow down. What's the rush?" he asked as she shoved her tongue down his throat.

"You said you wanted to show me something, but I think I need to show you something."

Her right hand slid into his boxers, pulling out nine and a half inches of pure meat. Her light blue eyes lit up like firecrackers on the Fourth of July when she saw what she had in her hands.

"You sure you can handle all of this?"

"I don't know, but I'm gonna have so much fun trying," she mumbled as she suddenly fell to her knees. Moments later her mouth was infused with his erection, sliding back and forth inside her tender, sweet mouth. She was taking his full length and girth like it was nothing, sucking and swallowing, acting as if she had known him her whole life.

The pleasurable noises she made caused Twan to grab her by the neck and pull her up off him.

"Hey, you making too much noise down there."

"I can't help it—it's a damn mouthful."

"I know. Here, let me just hit that ass from the back."

Her eyes widened. "What, you wanna fuck me in my ass?"

A side smirk crossed his face. "No, silly. I'm gonna tear a hole in that tight pussy of yours."

"Oh, my bad," she replied as she slid her panties down, revealing a nice, completely shaven pussy. He lifted her up, placing her ass over the sink. Slowly, he pulled her legs apart, staring at what he'd been waiting to see.

"There it is," he mumbled, shaking his head from side to side.

"What is it?"

"Nothing, baby girl. But you might wanna put your arms over my shoulders."

"Why?" she asked innocently.

"Because, truth be told, you're about to enter a world you've never been in before. Your little womb is about to be engulfed by a whole lot of dick."

"Are you serious?" she asked, mouth agape.

"Hell yeah. Think it's a motherfucking joke if you want to." He whispered into her ear, "I'm 'bout to tear this pussy up."

She looked into his brown eyes. "Okay. Put my arms over your shoulders like this?" She wrapped her arms around him, her heart racing like a horse in the Kentucky Derby.

"Yeah. Now hold on tight while I push this beast up in that tight pussy."

"How you know it's tight?"

"I can just tell, sweetheart."

"How?" she whispered, sounding sexy.

"Just call me a pussy connoisseur," he said with a devilish smile.

"Well, be gentle with me, please."

"Don't worry."

He rubbed his large dickhead against her sex walls, then paused.

"Have you ever been with a black guy before?" he asked, stiff in his hand.

"No. I haven't been with a black man, nor a white man. I'm still a virgin."

"Yep, I knew it."

"Is something wrong?"

"Nah. Just hold on."

He gently pushed inside her. At first she fidgeted, pretending it didn't hurt. Twan pulled her closer.

"Unh, umn. You better take this dick," he said, pushing in the tip.

As half of his tip slid inside, she tried to scream. Thinking fast, he stuck his tongue down her throat.

"Umm, umm," she moaned as he went deeper.

"Oh my God, what are you putting inside me—your fucking arm?"

He smirked and kept pushing. "No, baby, it's this dick. I told your little hot ass I was gonna show you something you've never seen before."

"Damn, it feels like you're inside my stomach already," she whimpered as a tear slid down her face.

"I know, right. Just hold tight, baby girl, I'm about to get there." He pushed deeper.

The sensation soon turned to pleasure as her hips began to gyrate with his every movement.

"You okay?"

"Yes, I guess I can handle it, huh?"

"I guess so, but that's not all of it—that's just half this dick."

Her secretions coated him, causing him to plunge the rest of his length deep inside. She clung to his neck, pulling him forward as he dug deeper and deeper.

"Oh shit!" she chirped.

"What?"

"I think I just had an orgasm," she cried, tears in her eyes.

"Don't worry, you'll have two before I'm done with this tight pussy," he spat.

"Oh goodness, I think I just had two more, back-to-back. Don't stop. Go deeper," she whispered.

Twan grabbed both her ass cheeks and pushed as deep as he could.

"Damn, baby, I think I done hit bottom."

"I know. I feel it too," she said as he continued, sliding in circles.

Ten grueling minutes later, he burst his second nut inside her, then slowly pulled out after making sure he shot his full load. When she saw a little cum still on his tip, she said, "Oh no, we can't have that."

She hopped off the sink, dropped to her knees, and caught every last drop in her open mouth.

Twan sluggishly looked down, almost falling from the weakness in his legs. His knees buckled.

"Damn, you a fucking pro at this dick-sucking shit, huh?" he asked, back against the bathroom door.

She smiled up at him. "No, Daddy. I just didn't want any of our kids to hit the floor."

"Kids? Who said anything about having kids?" he mumbled to himself as he fixed his clothes.

Chapter 13
Compromising Situation!

Now I know a few of y'all are saying to yourselves that I was a very insensitive young man for sleeping with one of my number-one females in the group. But ask yourself, *what would you have done in my compromising situation?* Your answer would always be the same—*"Hell yeah, I would've fucked the dog shit out of her fine red ass!"* And that's exactly what I had done, as I lay there watching her ass slide back up her thongs.

"So you know we have to keep this between you and me, right?" she asked as she tied up her gown.

"I already know, Mignon. You must don't remember what Rhynyia shouted right before she left the other night?" I asked, her words playing back in my head.

"How could I forget? She had just stuck her head out of that ambulance and shouted out to us, *'Alright ladies, until I return, you bitches be good and take care of my muthafuckin' man! And please don't make me come back and fuck one of y'all up for fuckin' his black ass!'*"

"So yes, Michael, I can still hear her words ringing in my ear as I stand here."

"I know, right? I can damn well hear them too," I replied as I lay there in the same bed where I had fucked many women before Mignon.

"So why did we both cross that line then, Michael?" she asked as she eased closer to the bed.

She sat right next to me, gazing in my face, waiting for an answer.

"I guess when the heart wants what it wants, you gotta give it to it," I whispered.

"So you're telling me your heart wants me just as much as my aching heart wants you?" she asked, her gorgeous eyes beginning to water.

"I guess so, Mignon," I told her. She placed her soft hand on my waist, then moved up until she had my half-erected penis in her hand.

"Well, let me show you how much me and my heart really want you," she voiced as she leaned over and placed her warm mouth over the head of my manhood.

"Oh shit!" I muttered, caught by surprise. At first, I tried to resist, mumbling, "No, Mignon, you don't have t—"

It was too late. The sensation of her mouth and the sight of her head going up and down had me spent...

***

Now back to your girl Lil Kitty. Even though she was cute and attractive, she wasn't stupid. Ever since we got back into town that dreadful weekend, she'd been trying to put two and two together. First, Punkin stood her up. Then, all of a sudden, he wanted to see her. But every time she received a call or text from his ass, it was never him directly.

"Something is off about this whole thing. Why isn't this nigga calling me so I can hear his voice?" she asked herself as she sat on her bed, in the middle of doing her hair for the show.

"Let me call my girl, Chyna," she said out loud just as her phone rang. When she reached for it, she couldn't believe who was on the caller ID.

"Damn girl, I was just about to call you," she said into the phone.

"What, so you could tell me about what happened to them niggas in Jacksonville over the weekend?" Chyna asked.

"Nah, what happened over the weekend?" Kitty asked, staring at herself in her full-length mirror.

Chyna sighed before answering. "Girl, how 'bout they found a group of niggas dead inside that same warehouse where them lame-ass niggas took me and White Chocolate."

"What? Did they say who they were?" Lil Kitty asked, a bad feeling washing over her petite frame.

"All I know is one of the niggas I vibe with up there said it was some dudes they seen some of our girls talking to," Chyna told her.

"Oh my God, I can't believe what I'm hearing," Kitty muttered, sitting down on her bed, gathering her thoughts. *Could one of those dead men be my Punkin?*

"Hey, do you know what a guy named Punkin looks like?" she asked, mind racing.

"Yeah, I think he was the short nigga I saw your girl Mignon talking to," Chyna answered with assurance.

All Kitty could do now was envision Mignon—or any of the other girls she assumed were The Murder Queens— pulling the trigger on her man.

"Hey, you still there?" Chyna asked, hearing only silence.

"Oh yeah, I'm still here, chick. Just thinking," Kitty quickly spat.

"Well, while you're doing that, let me handle something real quick."

"What's more important than helping me piece together this murder mystery?" Kitty asked.

"I really can't speak on it right now, Kitty, but believe me—when this shit hits the fan, you're gonna be right dab smack in the middle of it."

"That serious, huh?"

"As serious as a muthafuckin' heart attack," Chyna said, her malice toward me and the group building up inside her.

"Well, before you go, do you think Mike and them few girls that be by his side are up to no good?"

"All I know, Lil Kitty, is the words Suga Bear spoke a few months ago seem suspiciously true."

"What words were those? You know that bitch always got something slick to say. Matter of fact, her Suga Bear lookin' ass got one more time to come out her mouth sideways, and I'm gonna be on that ass like white on rice," Kitty snapped.

"Yeah, right, Lil Kitty," Chyna mumbled to herself, then said, "You don't remember that day in the limo when she told Mike that The Murder Queens didn't come to fruition until The Florida Hot Girls came on the scene?"

"Oh snap! You're absolutely right!" Kitty said with conviction, leaping off the bed like she hit the lotto.

"I know I am. Now let me do what I gotta do."

"Go ahead and do you, while I call Mike and ask his black ass a few questions. He was supposed to speak to me last night about some things but never got around to it."

"That's Mike for you," Chyna said as she ended the call.

Just as she did, the heifer dialed the number to the one agency I never imagined her calling. The phone rang twice before a female voice answered—

"Jacksonville…"

Chapter 14
Mykel!

While Chyna was busy doing that, one thing was certain—her actions would put Lil Kitty dead smack in the middle of it all when the shit hit the fan. It was as if Chyna could see into the future, because in just a few days, all hell was about to break loose for me and my precious Florida Hot Girls. If only I had seen it coming, I would've never taken my stable of women up to Jacksonville on that dreadful weekend...

***

I still couldn't get over how Mignon had walked into my bedroom and let me have my way with her. Not only had I made love to her, but I had made love to her mouth as well. Now I sat to myself with just a tad of remorse. Not only had I crossed the line with her, but I had broken the bond between her and Rhynyia.

What had I done? If Rhynyia found out, I knew for a fact she wouldn't allow Mignon to walk the face of this green earth. She would hunt her down for her lustful mistake— right after telling me it was over between us. All this played out in my head as I walked out of the bathroom, fresh from a shower. Sitting back on my bed, I thought of the repercussions for my careless actions.

"She just won't find out," I mumbled to myself, glancing at my nightstand. My phone lit up with an incoming call from hot-ass Lil Kitty.

"Not right now, Kitty, not right now," I said out loud, still relishing the good night I'd had at the club. I had money bulging from every pocket of my silk pants, sprawled across one of my bedroom chairs.

It was midday when I ventured downstairs to fix something to eat. Just as I opened the refrigerator, the damn doorbell rang out loud.

"Damn," I whispered, peeping out the door to see none other than the beautiful little face of my baby girl, Mykel, standing next to her mother, Tamika.

"Good morning—or should I say good afternoon?" Tamika said as I opened the door in surprise.

I glanced at my watch, then back into her cute face. "Afternoon, you two," I said, wondering what I had done to earn the pleasure of them stopping by on a school day.

"Well, for starters, your daughter here has been waiting on you to call her. Since you didn't, she asked me to bring her over," Tamika said.

"Come on in," I told them as they walked past me like I was the doorman.

Lil Mykel walked in enthusiastically, like a kid at the county fair, keeping her eyes trained on me the whole time.

"Here, have a seat."

"Thank you," Tamika said, as Mykel sat to her left, still watching me.

"So, Mykel, how are you doing? And why aren't you in school today?" I asked.

She looked at her mother, then back at me before hesitating. Tamika stared her down. "Go ahead, tell your father why you're not in school."

Mykel gazed into my eyes, looking just like her older sister, Shakina. "Well, first of all, Dad, I'm fine. Second, I punched this boy in the face for putting his hands in my hair."

"You what?" I slid up in my chair to look at her.

"Yes, Michael. And that's just the beginning of it—they suspended her lil' grown ass for three days."

"I see," I said, staring back into her small eyes. "So, why is she here?"

Tamika answered calmly. "I think she should stay with you for a while, so she can learn some discipline."

I had to stand up at that point. When I heard Tamika say something about Mykel staying with me, I thought she was speaking German. Not even my first wife, Carrie Lou, ever asked me to keep my first daughter for a few days. Hell nah—especially if she'd known about all the women living with me.

"Michael! Do you hear me talking to you?" Tamika snapped, pulling me back to reality.

"Oh yeah, my bad," I said, looking down at quiet little Mykel. I didn't know if I was angry or frustrated by what her mother had just said. All I knew was that my daughter had been suspended, and at a time like this, she needed her absent father more than anything.

As I turned toward her, walking slowly to the window, she didn't know whether to look at me or turn away. I knew she needed me—and honestly, at that point in my complicated life, I needed her too. She was my baby girl. What kind of father would I be to say no?

It would be years later, while locked away in prison, that I'd think back to this moment. I had reached out to Shakina, my oldest, trying to call her. She never picked up. So I sent her an email that simply read:

"Gee, I've been trying to reach you all day, but for some strange reason, you won't pick up the phone. Boy, where are a father's kids when he needs them the most?"

Her reply was short, but to this day it still haunts me. She wrote back:

"What do you tell a four-year-old girl, who waits in the window, wondering when, or if ever, her father will come back home?"

Every time I play that back in my head, I wish I had stuck around to see all my kids become adults.

Turning back to Tamika, the first thing I said was, "Wait a minute—you know my schedule. And besides, you said you didn't want her around all my female employees."

Then, out of nowhere, lil' precious Mykel jumped up and shouted, "Dad, you don't have to worry about me. I already know about the girls you have working for you. My brother told me the other day that you're a pimp!"

Tamika and I turned our heads toward each other, then back at Mykel with shocked looks.

"Mykel, what did you just say?" I asked as she snickered.

"My brother told me you're a pimp—whatever that means."

"Oh my goodness, these kids today are growing up too fast," Tamika said, hands on her hips, while Mykel stood waiting on an answer about staying with me.

I kneeled down in front of her. "First of all, young lady, I'm not a pimp."

"What's a pimp, Dad?" she asked, staring directly into my eyes.

"Mykel, I have female dancers. Strippers. They perform at clubs and bachelor parties."

"Parties?" she said excitedly. "Can they come to my next birthday party?"

I laughed, stood up, and looked at her mother. "Not those types of parties, young lady. I'll explain everything later tonight."

"So, Michael, that means she can stay?" Tamika asked.

I couldn't say no—she was my daughter, the youngest of the three beautiful girls I had. I looked down at her gorgeous little reflection of me and said, "Of course she can stay. But I have a show tonight, and another on Friday."

"So who's going to watch her tonight?"

"Don't worry, I'll handle that. I'll drop her back off Friday."

"That's fine," Tamika replied, looking down at our daughter. "You be good, okay?"

"Yes ma'am," Mykel said, hugging her. As soon as she did, Tamika was out the door, backing her car out the driveway.

I looked over at my little princess. "Have you had anything to eat yet, young lady?"

"I ate some carrot curls at lunch, Dad, but nothing else."

"Carrot curls?" I asked, puzzled.

"Yes sir. I don't like the food they serve at school, so I just nibble on vegetables until I get home."

Chapter 15
Follow Them!

While me and my youngest daughter got acquainted with one another, the flight my brother and his two henchmen were on had just landed in San Juan, Puerto Rico. Their flight touched down around 2:20 p.m. They looked like three businessmen as they strutted through the airport. Once they emerged outside, they made their way over to a convoy of black Range Rovers parked in front of the airport. Just as they walked up on the vehicles, a large bodyguard emerged, causing them to halt dead in their tracks. Then, as if she was summoned on cue, she revealed herself with a side smirk on her face.

"Welcome back to Puerto Rico, Señor Vallentino," Countess said as she greeted my brother with a shy smile.

"Hello, Countess, it is, right?" he asked curiously.

"Yes, it's Countess. You're aware of the accident with my sisters onboard, correct?"

"Yes. I spoke with your father and he told me the sad news. Have they been found yet?" he asked, while Twan and Fabian stood silent, not knowing what was going on.

"Not yet, but they will be found. One thing I know about my sisters—they've got a great deal of resilience inside of them. It runs in our family. Now we must be going." She motioned for the men to step inside the Range Rover. When they were seated, she gave the order.

"We can leave now."

The driver shifted into drive and pulled off. Twan and Fabian looked spooked—not just by her gorgeous appearance but by the large number of bodyguards with her.

"Damn, Smooth, where the ladies for my brother and me?" Fabian asked, gazing at the radiant young woman.

"Patience, my dear boy. Patience," he said, while Countess noticed the bewilderment in their eyes.

"Oh, I'm so sorry. Forgive me—where are my manners? Let me introduce myself." She extended her manicured hand, taking Fabian's softly. "I'm Countess Santiago." Her face still didn't reveal a full smile.

"Nice to meet you," the brothers said, still unable to believe how beautiful she looked.

"Me as well," she replied.

A few cars behind the convoy, a lone car watched. Inside, a distressed man in the passenger seat looked over at the driver.

"Follow them!"

"Yes, sir." The driver did as he was told, while Countess looked down at her timepiece.

"We need to make good time—we don't want to upset the man of the hour."

"Yes, Countess," the bodyguard in the passenger seat replied.

"Excuse me—man of the hour?" Fabian asked, his eyes roaming the sedan.

"That would be my father."

"Oh, no problem. I thought we had to meet someone else."

"No. The only person you'll be meeting here is my father, Pierre Santiago," she said, reciting his name like he was the damn president.

"Yeah, I told y'all about him before we left," Firstborn said, glancing at Fabian, wondering why it mattered. He was the hired help, not the H.N.I.C.

"Well, since we got that out the way, who the other guys following behind us, trying to keep their distance?" Twan asked, pointing at a black sedan four car lengths back.

"Where?" Countess asked, her head snapping around...

Meanwhile, in Duval, Trigger was busy putting together a team of cold-blooded killers. He was even thinking of a name to call them. Right now, all he had was his right-hand man, Cheese, seated in the passenger seat still trying to reach Lil Breezy.

"So what's good, my man—still not answering his phone?" Cheese asked dully.

"Nah, son, and that just don't make no fuckin' sense. That lil ass nigga should be answering by now," Trigger said, a gloomy look on his face.

"I hate to tell you this, fam..."

"Tell me what, Trigger?" Cheese asked, his eyes watering.

"I believe them fools went down to Orlando and got themselves killed."

"Nah, man! Don't say that shit, my nigga!" Cheese shouted, angry and frustrated.

"There's no other way to say it, fam. Them niggas had to go down there and got they stupid asses whacked! Think about it—why else that lil nigga not answering?" Trigger said as he pulled into the projects. They were there to meet up with a nigga named Big Country. He was a wild boy, real hood, loved to play with guns. Killing people was right up his alley. If only he'd been advised of what and who he was about to be up against, maybe his story would've ended different.

Just as Trigger parked, he reached over and put his hand on his partner's back.

"Listen, man, stop all that crying and shit. Save that shit for them niggas' funeral this weekend."

"But how we gon' have a funeral if we don't know if them niggas dead?" Cheese asked, teary-eyed.

"I ain't talking about Lil Breezy and his cousin Breezy. I'm talking about Punkin and his crew."

"Oh, my bad," Cheese said, drying his eyes.

"Now check this out. You stay your sentimental ass out here in the car while I go holla at this nigga. We gon' need his help if we want to get at these hoes going around whacking niggas like us."

"I hear you," Cheese said as he dapped his boy up, then watched Trigger step out.

Trigger hadn't even made it inside the man's apartment before Cheese decided to make a call—a call that would drastically change the lives of the few men Trigger thought he was putting together to bring the Murder Queens to their death...

***

Back in Orlando, Marc Dawg had left the hotel and was headed to the crib—he needed a shower and a change of clothes. As he drove home, he couldn't help but laugh at what he just did. Last night was a blur; all he remembered was the fantastic time he had with the two strippers he'd fucked for free, leaving both of them back at the hotel waiting for money and breakfast.

"Damn, lil shorty was thick as a fuckin' Snickers!" he thought to himself. He was on Orange Blossom Trail, mad thoughts rolling through his dazed mind. The female he was daydreaming about was the lil redbone he'd left in bed.

"I should've woke that bitch up and told her ass to ride with me. That way I could've left that other dick-suckin' hoe there all by her lonesome!" he said out loud, running straight through a red light—without seeing the police cruiser ducked off at a convenience store, waiting for a young brother like Marc Dawg to fuck up.

He still didn't notice the cruiser as it pulled out behind him, running the North Carolina license plate...

Chapter 16
Rescued!

The crew of Pierre's private jet didn't know how long they'd been floating in the open ocean. Neither did they know where one of the members was as they looked around at one another. All they did know was that, at the present moment, they were safe and sound. The island they'd washed up on was small, with a handful of trees. Some trees had fruit; others were bare.

"Is there any chance of us being rescued?" Maria asked Miguel, who still seemed shaken.

"I have no idea. The plane was equipped with a homing device just weeks ago." He said, sitting up onto his knees.

"So my father must know that something terrible has happened to us by now!" Natasha voiced, somewhat frightened as she stood.

"Let's hope so. Now where is Rhynyia?" Maria asked, sitting in the dry sand. She had one shoe on; the other was in her hand.

"I thought she was the one who helped us out of the water—right before we were eaten by the sharks." Natasha said, placing her right hand over her eyes. Then she frantically began shouting for her sister. "Rhynyia! Rhynyia! Rhynyia, answer me!"

They waited to hear something but heard nothing but the wind blowing through the trees.

"She has to be on the island. There's no way she was killed by those sharks," Miguel said, trying to sound convincing. But deep down he knew the truth of what had happened to her.

"I tell you what—break off into three groups and search for her. She has to be here somewhere; there's no way in hell she isn't!" Natasha screamed. She desperately needed to find her sister.

"Yes, Natasha. We're on it right now!" Maria said as she rose to her feet. Needless to say, Maria was like the mother Rhynyia never had—she'd agreed years ago to travel and help Rhynyia find her long-lost mother. Now, years later, she was on a small island searching for the young woman she'd sworn to protect with her life.

"Listen—meet back here in forty-five minutes!"

"Yes, Natasha!" Miguel and Maria said in unison as everyone went in different directions with one thing on their minds. They all had to find Rhynyia, no matter what.

***

Just a few miles away, on a small boat, were two people. They weren't out fishing like on other days; they were looking to rescue whoever had crashed in the ocean.

"Do you think whoever crashed is still alive, father?" the young man asked.

"I have no idea, my son. I just hope and pray they're still alive," his father replied as he saw what looked like a small sand dune up ahead. "Look—look! Up in the distance!"

The young lad stood in the boat and saw what his father pointed at. "I see it!" he exclaimed with joy. "Do you think what I'm thinking?"

"Let's hope and pray whoever crashed is there." His father sped up; he wanted to get there to render much-needed help.

***

Back at the Vallentino estate, I'd taken Mykel by her small hand and led her toward the kitchen. I was still taken back to my old school days as I told her.

"Yes, I can still remember those days of that horrid food."

"It's not all that bad. I can deal with it sometimes, but my greedy brother eats up everything." She said, standing in my kitchen and looking around as if amazed at the large room. I could tell she was surprised at how big my home was.

"So, Dad, you live up in this big ole house with a lot of girls?" she asked, sitting on a bar stool behind the bar.

"Yes, baby girl, I do. And make sure you tell your little mannish brother I'm not a pimp." She smiled and reached for a handful of grapes in a bowl next to her.

"Whatever, Dad." She spoke quickly, chewing the grapes. "Now where is my room, or am I sleeping in your room?"

I smiled as I turned around, about to fix her something to eat. "You sure do have a lot of questions, don't you, young lady?"

"How am I supposed to know anything if I don't ask?"

"You're right. You will be sleeping in your own room. As soon as I fix you a sandwich, I'll show you up."

"I hope it's big like everything else in this big ole house."

"Yes, it's big enough for you." I replied, standing there trying to figure out what I was going to do with her for the next few days. Part of me was happy to have her around, while the dawg in me worried what would happen if Sharon decided to stop by. How would I explain my little bundle of joy to her—who at that moment was stealing my heart? And with this new news told to an unexpected Sharon, how sure was I that it wouldn't break her heart in the process?

Chapter 17
A Rat Amongst Us

The number he dialed belonged to a man who had a lot at stake in what was transpiring up in Duval. If Cheese hadn't made the call, a lot of innocent people might have lost their lives because of what was being put together.

The mystery person's phone rang twice before a smooth male voice picked up. "Yeah, what's popping?"

"It's going down right now," Cheese said into the phone.

"So you say. What's his plan?" the voice asked.

Cheese eased up in his seat and looked carefully around—he wanted to make sure his surroundings were safe enough to talk. "Right now we're over at what looks like some run-down apartments."

"Okay, where is the nigga?" the voice asked as he stood in his kitchen, leaned up against the refrigerator.

"He's inside one of the apartments, talking with some cat who calls himself Big Country," Cheese said as he pulled out a smoke. His nerves were all over the place.

"I see. Tell you what—once he has all his people in place, call me back." The person on the other line said, then disconnected.

"Hello, hello—this cool ass nigga done hung up," Cheese mumbled to himself as he closed his phone.

He never wanted anything to do with what was going on between a few no-good niggas in Duval and some bad-ass strippers from Orlando, FL. But when he accidentally overheard two cats early one morning bragging about taking two females from Orlando to a warehouse and forcing one of them to suck his dick, he instantly thought about his own flesh and blood.

After what happened to Chyna and White Chocolate that terrible weekend, local female strippers from the Duval area started coming up missing. A few days later, their naked bodies were found—most had been raped and tortured before being murdered. Cheese had a soft spot for those women who danced for all types of reasons. No one should be killed for what they did, even if they were strippers. They still didn't have to die the way they did.

This hurt Cheese deeply—he'd lost his only sister at the hands of the person who went around killing these women. He vowed an oath to seek revenge, just like The Murder Queens had begun to do. Don't get it twisted—Cheese didn't know The Murder Queens nor any members of the dance group called The Florida Hot Girls. But he'd seen a few of them shopping one day at the Golf Fair Flea Market. That's where he'd bumped into one of them. He'd been smitten by her beauty, became infatuated, they exchanged numbers, and the rest was history.

***

Inside the run-down apartment, your boy Trigger was growing impatient with the big fella. It had been thirty minutes since the man's elderly grandmother opened the door and let him in. Big Country had gone to take a shower.

"Damn, my man—how long you gonna be in there?" Trigger asked from the small living room.

"Yo fam, give me about another fifteen!" Big Country shouted as he washed his funky ass.

"He always takes long-ass showers. Round here got my water bill high as my fucking rent!" his eighty-year-old grandmother grumbled as she walked toward her bedroom. "I can't wait until his big sorry ass moves the fuck out of my house!" she muttered, then turned back to stare at Trigger. He didn't know what to say as the elderly woman sized him up. "So you're here to give his sorry ass a job?"

"Something like that, ma'am," he replied quietly.

"I sure hope so, even though he's a big ass baby. That's still my fucking grandson." She walked into her bedroom.

Truth be told, Big Country was her heart ever since his father got himself killed one night while shooting dice. His father had crapped out—losing all his money. When Danny Boy realized he'd lost everything, he grabbed the money and ran. The sad thing about his dumb mistake was he never figured on a young ass nigga named Cheese running behind him and shooting him in the back.

Trigger stood and gazed at pictures aligned on the wall. He hadn't even heard Big Country walk up behind him. "Sorry about that, fam. What's hood?" Trigger turned to face the giant.

"Damn, how long do you need to take a shower?" Trigger asked him.

Big Country stood 6'4" and weighed around two hundred fifty pounds—a high-yellow brother with red hair he wore in a small afro. When it wasn't in an afro, he'd braid it up in small braids.

"My bad, fam. Had to wash these nuts," he replied with a smirk.

"I don't know why your big sorry ass ain't fucking no hoes," Trigger said.

"Nigga please. Yo boy round her fucking all these hoes," Big Country defended.

"Whatever, nigga—I know you didn't drive all the way over here to check how many hoes I'm fucking!" Trigger continued.

"Nah son, I didn't. What I come to talk to you about is some serious business," Big Country said.

"Word."

"Yes sir—this shit is right up your alley," Trigger said with a gleam in his eyes.

"Nigga, say it then—who we 'bout to murk?" Big Country asked, heart and mind intensifying. He lived for the kill. But like I told you earlier—if he'd been warned about who he was about to go up against, he might've had second thoughts about signing his own death certificate.

***

Countess quickly leaped into action—she had a keen eye for observation. She spotted a black sedan following about four car links behind them. Her head spun around to the front.

"We have ourselves a tail, Manuel—lose them!"

"Yes, Countess—right away," he shouted.

"So, who do you think it is?" Firstborn asked nervously, eyes locked on Countess but his mind on how, before they'd left Puerto Rico, they'd been in the middle of a gunfight. In that situation he'd been with Natasha while I was with Rhynyia.

"I haven't the slightest. Were you guys followed at the airport?" she asked, preparing for the worst.

"No, not that I can think of," he said as she looked over at the brothers. "Did you guys see anything out of the ordinary?"

"Nah, not really," they both replied in unison.

"It doesn't matter now. I have to call my father," Countess said, reaching for her phone. Just as she had it in her hand, her head turned to see if the car was still behind them.

To her surprise, it was closer now, looking as if the people inside were preparing for an attack. Her father's phone rang once before he answered. "Yes, my dear," he said, sounding like a man without a care in the world—not like a man whose family was suffering death at an alarming rate.

"Someone is following us."

"Did you get a good look at them?"

"No sir, by the car I can't tell if they're locals or the police."

"It's not the police. I can assure you of that, my dear," he replied, listening to his daughter.

"How can you be so sure they're not the police, Father?" she asked.

"Because I pay them too much to be after some two-bit local drug dealer who doesn't know what he's gotten himself and his family involved in," he told her.

If I had known how Pierre really felt about my brother and my immediate family, I would've traveled to Puerto Rico myself and put a lone bullet right between his eyes before he gave my brother more kilos of dope to push.

Chapter 18
Blam! Blam! Blam!

"I see," Countess recited as she kept her eye on the traffic following them, then looked over at Firstborn—without him knowing what her father had just said about him and his family. It wasn't until she heard her father's voice in her ear that she understood.

"It has to be the people responsible for Naheed's death. Have the driver cause some type of accident, then do what you've been taught to do."

"Yes, Father! Once it's over I shall call you back."

"No—once the deed is done, get to the yacht. I have too much money at stake." The phone hung up without him even saying goodbye. She mumbled a few words and hung up as well. "Cause some type of accident. Once the traffic behind us comes to a stop, circle back around. I'll take it from there," she told the driver while making sure her Glock 30 was fully loaded. Twan and his brother's eyes almost bulged as they watched her put in the extended clip.

"Yes, señorita." The driver obeyed, running a red light and causing the few cars behind them to slam on their brakes. Just as the two rear Range Rovers cleared, Manuel yelled out the window, "Get to the yacht—we'll be there within minutes!"

"What about the passengers?" the other driver shouted.

"Just do as I said! We will be there momentarily! Just get to the yacht, now!" The two Range Rovers sped away as sirens sounded in the distance.

"Circle the accident now!" Countess yelled.

"What are you going to do?" Firstborn frantically asked, sitting on pins and needles.

Countess wore the fierce look of a lioness. "Just sit still while I do what I do best." She reached for a red bandanna and wrapped it around her face. As the vehicle circled, she leaped out with her weapon in hand and ran up on the unsuspecting black sedan. By the time the driver realized what was taking place, it was too late. What the two men heard next was what the local police in San Juan would later call a horrific crime in the middle of the mean streets of Puerto Rico.

Blam! Blam! Blam! Blam!

The passenger in the sedan had no time to react as he wildly threw his hands up trying to stop the first bullet, but it was no use—the bullet tore off the front portion of his skull, making it look like a Volkswagen Beetle convertible. Two more rounds hit the partially bald man dead center in the chest. The other two rounds were fired into the air to keep the man in the back seat at bay.

"Oh shit!" the remaining passenger shouted as he leaped from the car, trying to avoid the onslaught. His attempt to hide was no use; Countess swiftly walked around to where he crouched. Tears flooded his eyes as he threw his hands up and shouted, "No, no, no—please! I have a family!"

"Who sent you?" she asked, anger burning on her face.

"I can't—he will kill me and my family!" the frightened man yelled, hiding his face.

The man was still near the car, thinking he had escaped. Just as he saw his chance, he dashed for the door. "Boom, boom, boom!" Countess hit him in the back three times before he fell face-first, dead.

Tears that had formed in the man's eyes now flowed down his face as he saw the last of his partners dead. "Now that he's dead, do you want to join him?"

"No—no!" he cried.

"So what in the hell do you think I'm going to do—just let you walk away scot-free?" she barked as sirens drew nearer.

"I would hope and pray you would, señorita. Please spare my life," he begged.

"Why? So you and whoever you work for can kill me and my remaining family members later on down the road?" she asked.

Her driver stepped to the rear of the Rover and shouted, "Countess, the police are getting closer—we must go now!" She turned her head as if on a swivel. "Grab him—he's coming with us."

"Are you sure?" the driver asked.

Her mean stare answered before she spoke. "Yes. If he won't tell me what I want to know, I'm pretty sure he'll tell my father once he sees what he has in store for him." The driver briskly swept the man up, knocking him out, then secured him tightly in the back seat.

Firstborn and his henchmen watched the beaten man before Firstborn asked Countess, "So what, we taking hostages now?"

"No, smart ass. If he won't tell me what I want to know, when he sees what my father has in store for him, he'll tell him everything—plus some more." She looked at the driver. "Get us to the yacht before the police get here."

The driver wasted no time. As soon as the vehicle pulled up, the other guards were already waiting. "Hurry! We must leave before anyone can follow us," Countess yelled as she stepped onto the luxurious yacht.

"You don't have to tell me twice," Firstborn said, stepping right behind her, almost trampling her.

"What about him?" the first guard asked.

"Make sure his ass is tied up and throw him in the back. We have a special place for men who don't want to talk," she ordered.

"Damn, what do you think they're going to do to him?" Twan whispered to his brother, who was busy trying not to get in the way of the movement on the prestigious vessel.

"I have no idea, baby brother, but I'm pretty damn sure we're about to find out," Fabian said as he stepped onto the expensive vessel.

"Make yourselves comfortable—eat and drink whatever you like. Just not too much," Countess told them as she moved about the boat.

"Why did she say that?" Fabian asked Firstborn, leaning over him.

"I have not a clue," Firstborn replied, reaching for a few handfuls of shrimp, then moving to the crabs before looking at his main man. "But you'll find out before I do," he finished with a smirk, reaching for a glass of red wine—a taste that had become his favorite and, as time would prove, one of his downfalls.

If I could go back and undo everything I'd started, I would. But like one of my favorite rappers said in his song "Thinking Out Loud":

I would pick up the phone and call him—but I can't call him unless they make a time machine. That's a problem I can't solve.

—Moneybagg Yo

Chapter 19
Paintings!

Right after I watched my young daughter gobble down her food, I had to ask, "Do you want me to make you another sandwich since you ate that one so fast?"

"No sir," she replied, drinking a cup of orange juice. After she set the cup down, she gazed at me with those eyes of hers. "I ate it fast because you were standing there watching me eat it like you wanted some of it too." I couldn't do nothing but laugh at her smart-mouth comment. "Come on, girl—with your smart mouth."

"Where are we going?" she asked, leaping off the bar stool. "I want to show you to your room." She ran a wide smile across her face. "That's what I'm talking about," I shouted with excitement in my voice.

As I led her down the extensive hallway, I could still see the amazement in her face as she looked at the different artwork I had aligned on the walls.

"So you painted these pictures on the wall, Dad?"

"No, young lady—those are priceless paintings by famous painters."

"Oh really? If you ask me, they just look like a bunch of stuff I could've painted," she said as we stood gazing at a few pictures.

"So you paint?" I asked as we continued toward the room where she would sleep.

"I only do a little scribble and scrabble, Dad."

"I see. So where are your paintings now?"

"I have some at school and some at home."

"Really?"

"Yes, sir."

"I would love to see them one day. Do you think you can paint some while you're here so I can hang them on my walls?"

"I guess—why not. Besides, they'd look a whole lot better than what you already have."

"Whatever." I looked down at her, still smiling. As I opened the door to her room, she excitedly asked, "So is this my room?"

"Yes, Princess—this is a room a beautiful young girl like you shall sleep in." Her smile and tears let me know she approved. "Wow! I wish my brother could be here to see how big my room is!" She let my hand go and ran inside the massive room, fit for a princess.

"Yeah, I wish he could be here too, Mykel " She turned to me just as she was about to jump onto the huge bed. "Why don't we call Mom and tell her to bring him over here with us?"

"Nah—some things in life are only meant for you to enjoy. Always remember that, okay?" I said, sitting on her bed and looking directly into her eyes. I needed her to understand that early.

"Yes, sir." She proceeded to jump up and down on her new bed, displaying how much she enjoyed having something of her very own. I stood in the doorway, watching her act like a kid on Christmas morning. If things were only that simple.

"Now how do I keep Sharon from finding out Mykel is my daughter?" I asked myself as she continued to play.

I loudly turned to walk to my room when she ran to the door behind me. "So where are you going now, Dad?" she asked with a sad face.

"Back to my room, sweetheart. There are a few things I need to work on." Truth be told, I had to find out about Rhynyia and her family.

"Okay, so what am I supposed to do all by myself?" she asked, frowning.

"I haven't the slightest idea, my darling. What did you want to do?"

"Well," she paused, then said, "I was thinking maybe we could do some shopping since I didn't bring my school clothes."

I looked at her for a minute and said, "Boy, you are really something else, aren't you?" Her cute little dimples formed as she smiled. "I am your daughter, right?" Her shoulders shrugged and I simply replied, "Yes."

"So that means I think just like you, Dad."

"Nah—you think like a grown-ass little person already."

"Grams always says she believes I've been here before."

"You know, she just might be right. You might have been here before and now come back in the body of a small child."

"How can one do that, Dad?" she asked with a serious face.

"It's just a phrase, young lady. Now let me go put on some appropriate clothing so I can take you shopping, okay?"

"Yes, sir."

Moments later we pulled out of the driveway headed to the mall. I'd just made a right turn off my street when I looked over and saw her sitting beside me in the front seat. "Wouldn't it be nice to have my other little angels here with us?" I thought as it dawned on me that I hadn't seen them in years...

Chapter 20
The Infamous!

By the time they arrived at the house, the mood and tension were down to a minimum. Countess turned to the men.

"Okay guys, follow me. My father is out back waiting on you all."

Twan nudged Fabian and whispered, "Man, this place is fucking huge. This guy must be a serious player in the drug game."

"Nah, his ass *is* the drug game," Firstborn voiced as they all walked around the house to the back where Pierre was waiting. He looked like he had just gotten off the phone. Guards were all around the house, positioned like he was expecting an army.

Firstborn was busy taking everything in—none of this was set up just a few days ago. He politely tapped Countess on the shoulder.

"Hey, what's up with all the heavily armed men?"

"Since you guys left there's been an attack on my father and his brothers. And I know you know the plane you guys were on crashed somewhere over the Atlantic?" She turned to face him as she spoke.

"Yeah, I know. About that—have they been found yet?"

"I'm not sure. But with everything going on, we had to beef up security for the family. And with what just happened at the airport, I'm pretty sure there's more to come."

"Damn." Firstborn mumbled.

"Ahh, Señor Vallentino, so nice to see that you made it back safe and sound, my friend!" Pierre said as he stood to greet him, face holding a fake ass smile. My not-so-smart brother fell for it.

"Yes, barely," he muttered.

"I heard there was trouble at the airport. Are you and your associates okay?" Pierre asked, like he really gave a damn about their black asses.

"Yes sir, we're fine. But the one lone victim you've got tied up seems a lil frightened."

"Yes, that he is. Just wait until he finds out what I have in store for him," Pierre said as he stared at his guards taking the battered man behind the barn where his workers packed product. "Countess, did he say who sent him?"

"No, father. He said whoever sent him would kill him and his family."

"I see." Pierre lit a cigar and yelled to one of the men carrying the hostage. "Raul, have our guests prepared for dinner. My children are starving. Once he gets a good look at them, we'll see where his loyalty remains."

"Yes, sir, at once!" Raul replied, then yelled something in broken Spanish.

"So, what did he mean by his children are starving? You guys aren't about to eat the man, are you?" Firstborn asked with a dumbfounded look.

"No, silly. Remember when I told you guys not too much?"

"Yeah," Twan stepped up.

"Well, my father has some pets he likes to feed his enemies to."

"What?" Fabian shouted, his face showing second thoughts about this new line of work.

"You'll see. Just be patient," Countess replied, whispering something in her father's ear before kissing his cheek and walking away. Pierre turned his attention back to the fellas.

"Now, who are these fine two gentlemen with you?"

Firstborn rubbed his hands together, looked Pierre in the eyes, then at his two young villains.

"These two men right here are my associates. I had to hire them to expedite your precious yayo."

Twan and Fabian immediately extended their hands as they laid eyes on the infamous Pierre Santiago.

Meanwhile, the play Chyna put in motion was a cold one. Cold as a winter day in November, right in the middle of Alaska. *Yeah, it was just that fucking cold.*

I guess she must have felt her tenure as a Florida Hot Girl was coming to an end. Truth is, that wasn't what was about to happen at all. Like I said in the beginning of this unique story—*you,* the female who decided to join the group, decided your own fate.

Up until the last day of me having the group, I never, ever fired anyone. The only people I can recall firing were my shitty ass security guards and my cousin.

It would be almost a decade later before I saw Chyna again. I remember it like yesterday. Now as I sit in my cell listening to Sam Cooke sing *A Change Is Gonna Come*— which had to be my father's favorite song—I can envision that day.

It was a Saturday afternoon, mild and humid. I was in Lake City, Florida, having lunch with a beautiful woman from Live Oak. That same night was one of my biggest talent shows yet for Big Boy Entertainment Group.

We were at Red Lobster, and I had just placed our order when I looked up and saw her face. Elegant. Gorgeous. This was a decade after I left Orlando and relocated to Winter Haven. Chyna and her man were seated a few tables away from me and my date. She still looked amazing—and yes, she still had those mouth-watering titties.

I wanted to go say hi, especially when I heard her shout out, "Hey look! It's my boy Mike, the owner of them bad ass females called The Florida Hot Girls!"

When I heard that, I knew it was Chyna. But instead of going over, I just waved, gave her a weak smile, and turned back to my date. Even though her actions years earlier caused some of the girls in the group to catch a case, I didn't hold ill feelings toward her. How could I? Her actions didn't stop me from becoming the man I became.

Now, I didn't have concrete evidence she did what I thought she did to me and the group. You readers might even ask, "How do you know it was her who told?"

I'd simply tell you: "She was faking it all along, I could feel it in my bones. I had a feeling she told when I felt it in my soul."

Just like I'd feel years later with a female named Honey. Lil Durk and Lil Baby said it best in their song *Still Hood* ...

Chapter 21
Lil Child Runnin Wild!

When the dispatcher came back over the radio telling the young rookie officer that the car was registered to one Clifford Bubb Watkins, aka Lil Breezy, he instantly assumed the worst and asked,

"Are there any warrants out for this man? Over?"

There was a slight pause in transmission. A few moments later, as he trailed the car, he heard what he wanted.

"There are three outstanding warrants for this young man, and he's considered to be armed and very dangerous! Over."

She hoped the rookie caught that last part. Whatever she might've felt about Lil Breezy being armed and dangerous didn't matter one bit—his black ass was already dead in the trunk, lying next to Big Breezy.

"10-4, over," the officer uttered as he went to hit the lights. But right before he did, the dispatcher advised him,

"Proceed with caution!"

The officer shouted out loud, "Did you get my last transmission? Over!"

The dispatcher came back with urgency in her voice. "I do copy, dispatch. Go ahead and send back up! Over."

He radioed back as he hit his siren, then flipped on the blue lights.

Whoop-whoop! The loud horn blared.

Up ahead in the Bonneville, Marc Dawg heard the sound no young Black man wants to hear. His head full of dreads snapped toward the rearview. When he saw the cop car, he shouted,

"Oh shit! What the fuck?"

The patrol car was right on his bumper. The cop could've pushed him off the road if he wanted. To the officer, it looked like Marc Dawg was about to pull over—his head was moving side to side inside the car. But what Marc Dawg was really doing was looking around to make sure everything was clean.

His movements made the cop mutter, "Oh yeah, you Black ass son of a bitch! You're probably looking for your gun!"

The officer smashed the gas, ramming the back of the car.

Up ahead, Marc Dawg told himself to stay calm, that everything was going to be okay. He had no other choice but to pull over. He hit the blinker and was about to stop when his heart damn near jumped out of his chest. A rush of emotions and pure adrenaline surged through his veins as he realized his fuck-up.

In his mind, he replayed her last words:

"Take them and their car over to the salvage yard and have everything destroyed!"

The feelings now were indescribable.

Back behind him, the cop was just about to step out of his car when Marc Dawg must've heard Curtis Mayfield playing in his head. The song was *Little Child Running Wild.*

Just as the music came on, he floored it and left the cop in his dust.

Scrrrrrrrrrrr! The Bonneville's tires screamed as Marc Dawg had no regard for the law, his safety, or anyone else's.

"Cracker, yo ass is about to be on a high-speed chase!" he shouted as he sped down Orange Blossom Trail.

His mind was scattered as he weaved through heavy traffic. No way was he letting this cop catch him—not with two dead bodies in the trunk.

As he got closer to Colonial Drive, he asked himself, "What do I do now?"

The slow-ass car he was driving couldn't outrun the police. His mind instantly told him: get to Mercy Drive. He knew a big-time dope boy from down south who was in the city for a few days and still owed him a favor.

Once he got there, he could ditch the car and deal with the consequences later. All that mattered was getting as far away from the cop as possible—before more joined the chase …

***

Right before the guys met up with Pierre, he had just hung up with his men—the same ones out hunting for his family members. They told him there'd been a report of some people rescued out in the ocean. Hope sparked, but before he got off the phone, he asked,

"So are they all alright?"

There was a slight pause.

"Hello?" he snapped.

"Right now we have no idea on their situation. We don't even know if it's our people," the man said.

"Well, find out. Don't call me back until you know for sure it's them."

"Si, Señor," his man answered, then hung up.

When Pierre turned to greet my brother, it was as if he didn't have a care in the world—but deep down, he feared the worst.

When Firstborn's two comrades shook hands with him, you couldn't tell if the boys were scared or just nervous as hell meeting the notorious drug lord.

"Nice to meet you, sir. And may I add, you have a very beautiful home," Fabian said, pulling his hand back and shaking off Pierre's crushing grip.

"We thank you, my young friend. Maybe one day you'll have the pleasure of owning a home of this magnitude," Pierre said, studying the three men.

Firstborn, standing slightly off to the side, sensed the awkwardness. He cleared his throat.

"Excuse me, Pierre. Before we go any further, here's the money from the sale of your precious product."

He handed Pierre a black duffel stuffed with cash from the yayo—and the two dead cops he'd helped dispose of...

Chapter 22
Slaughtering Of The Hogs!

Pierre looked at the bag, then back up at Firstborn.

"Is everything in order, my good man?" He had a side smile on his face as he took the bag, shaking it to hear the money inside.

"Yes, sir, everything should be there," Firstborn uttered, smiling back at Pierre, who then shouted out to one of his men.

"Felipe!"

The young man swiftly turned his way. "Yes sir."

"Please take this to my wife. Have her count it and report the total back to me."

"Yes, sir." The young man stood, then walked toward the rear of the villa.

"So, Pierre, about the next total of bricks that I will need to—"

Pierre cut him off quickly. "Before we discuss the next load of my precious product, please follow me to the rear of the building."

The three men looked at one another, wondering where they were being led. When they stepped around the rear of the barn, Fabian froze at the sight before him.

"What the fuck?" he shouted, hands flying up to cover his mouth.

The battered man Countess and the guards had dragged back was stripped naked, bleeding from head to toe, strung up high above an empty corral—like he was waiting for their arrival.

"Damn, what in the fuck are they about to do to the poor man?" Twan asked, standing next to Firstborn, who couldn't believe his eyes.

"I really don't know. I've never made it back here," Firstborn answered, pulling a silk handkerchief from his suit jacket to cover his mouth, not wanting the stench to enter his nostrils.

"I've smelt this before," Fabian whispered, glancing at his younger brother.

"Now that you mention it, Fabian, I have too. It smells like when we were kids, right before our grandfather would slaughter his hogs!"

"Precisely, my young men. The only difference is we are not slaughtering hogs—the hogs are about to be the ones doing the slaughtering. If his ass doesn't start talking, he'll wish he had."

Pierre's spit flew as he yelled, jabbing at the man with a long wooden rod.

"Damn, this some real sick shit," Fabian said, watching in fear.

"I guess this why ole girl didn't want us to eat that much," Twan muttered, his lunch rising in his throat.

"Guess so. Damn, what a fucked-up way to die. You don't see shit like this unless you're at the movies," Firstborn muttered, watching the man swing from the chain holding his limp body.

"It sure the hell is. If you think this is bad, wait until you see what he does to the ones who cross our father when it comes to his precious yayo and money," Countess recited as she walked up behind Firstborn, laying a hand on his shoulder …

***

Mad thoughts raced through Miguel's mind as he searched the small island for the one he knew was already dead. He knew because he was the last to see her—right before he pushed her into the water for the shark to feast on.

The sight replayed in his head until he broke down, crying uncontrollably, collapsing to his knees in the sand.

"Oh God, why me? Why did she have to fly the gotdamn plane over the Bermuda Triangle?" he screamed, anguish twisting his voice.

The pain and final image of Rhynyia tormented him. He remembered her reaching out for his hand before he leapt onto what was left of the plane. Then the shark took her, a pool of blood blooming in the water. He knew he had to paddle away before more sharks appeared—and feasted on him next.

He knew all of this when Natasha stood up calling Rhynyia's name. But there was no way he'd tell her or Maria what really happened. His secret would die with him. If Pierre ever found out, his death would come sooner than later.

"Rest in peace, my sweet Princess. Rest in peace," he whispered, staring into the vast ocean, fearing they might never be saved.

Just then he spotted what looked like a fishing boat speeding their way.

"What the—" he muttered, thinking his mind was playing tricks. He shaded his eyes from the blazing sun, squinting. Two people were waving anxiously from the distance.

They had been saved…

***

Big Country and Trigger dapped each other at the man's front door before Trigger headed back to his car.

Cheese had almost dozed off when he spotted Trigger and a high-yellow kid who looked familiar.

"Oh snap! That soft-looking ass nigga looks like the cat I shot in the back," he muttered just as Trigger pulled the door handle and slipped inside.

"Sorry it took so long, fam. The nigga was taking a shower."

"So what, you took one too?" Cheese joked.

"Nah, silly ass nigga. I had to wait until he got his nasty ass out. After that I put him down with the lick."

"I see. So what? Is he down or what?"

"Yeah, he wit it. But get this though—" Trigger said, turning the ignition and backing away from the projects.

"What's the problem?" Cheese asked, eyes locked on Big Country.

"Dude, how 'bout Duval County is a real fucked-up place to live."

"What makes you say that, fam?" Cheese asked, pulling a blunt from his pocket.

"My man Big Country told me after this is all over, he's gonna need our help finding who killed his pops."

Cheese didn't look surprised as he sparked the blunt. "Word. How'd his old man die?"

"Boy, Country said the coward shot his pops in the back, then rolled him over and shot him twice in the face."

"That's cold," Cheese said, remembering that day.

"Tell me about it. It was so cold his grandmother had to have a closed casket funeral for her only son."

"Yep, sounds like she's gonna have one for his big red ass too," Cheese mumbled.

"What was that, partner?"

"I was saying—whoever it was, when we find him, he's gonna have a closed casket funeral too."

"When did I say it was a him?" Trigger asked, side-eyeing him while Cheese sat back, slow-smoking his blunt.

"I feel you," Trigger muttered, though his eyes stayed fixed on his partner, who was already plotting how and when to kill Big Country before the truth came out.

You see, in Duval County, Cheese knew the streets talked. It was only a matter of time before someone dropped his name.

"So where you headed now?" Cheese probed, blowing smoke.

"I got this lil homie who knows how to get the right guns we gonna need."

"Cool. Drop me at my car. We'll hook up later," Cheese said.

"Say less, my nigga," Trigger replied, bending a right onto Beaver Street...

Chapter 23
Not Right Now!

Lil Kitty had been pondering over the notion to call me for at least an hour after she hung up with Chyna. But what she should've been doing was getting ready for the show that night. We had a show in Gainesville, FL with the up-and-coming rap group, the Ying Yang Twins. Truth be told, some of the ladies might not have been too thrilled about the show as much as I was, since it was a new rap group on the scene.

But I was, simply because it was another show where I could meet more individuals who would hopefully one day desire to render the Hot Girls' service. The more notoriety the group would garner, the more exposure I assumed would catapult the girls and me into complete superstardom.

Years later, as I sit here in my cell writing this book, I see just how gotdamn famous that train of thought got my black ass. While most of my team of women are still performing at strip clubs and various bachelor parties, I'm hidden away in some shitty-ass prison in Oakdale, Louisiana. All I can say is, when them Alphabet Boys really want you and then hide your ass, don't worry. They'll give you just what you want—right along with an ass load of prison time. Football numbers, just like many rappers rap about in their songs.

I'll never forget the quote Plies has in *100 Years*:

A Public Defender doesn't get you but a long trip.

And a judge sentences an innocent nigga without any guilt.

In the end they give a nigga a 100 years.

Have your mama leaving out the courtroom in tears.

In the end, when you have your life taken away from you, you don't know how it feels.

The day I arrived back from sentencing, a young cat who resided in the same cramped-up cell as me asked, "Damn G, how does someone do thirty years?"

When he asked me that simple-minded question, there just happened to be another brother in the cell with us. He kindly said, "Just like my man Plies said. You just do it."

And that's exactly what I'm doing.

As I sit back and reflect on that day, Lil Kitty's phone call snapped me out of my private moment with Mykel. I had been avoiding her ass all day and knew I'd have to speak with her at some point. So why not now?

"Hello, Lil Kitty?"

"Oh, you finally decided to answer your phone, huh?" she asked, sarcasm laced in her voice.

"My bad, Lil Kitty. You know I do need sleep and rest?" I answered back, sarcasm in mine as well.

The entire time, Mykel was watching every word that came out of my mouth.

"Yeah, whatever," she said, then continued. "About last night Mike. I thought you were going to speak with me about something?"

I knew what she was talking about, but there was no way I was about to have that conversation with her at that moment. "My bad, once the club began to get crowded, things slipped my mind," I told her, not wanting to get into a long drawn-out conversation about some lil dead-ass nigga named Punkin.

"That's why I'm calling you."

At that moment I thought she knew the man was dead and that I had something to do with it. I was silent for a minute until she continued. "You need to tell me what's really going on," she stated angrily.

Now here I was, sitting with loathing feelings about what had to be done about her special friend, so I told her, "Not right now Lil Kitty, we'll talk at the show tonight."

I could hear her sucking her teeth in the background. "There you go! Well we need to hurry up and talk then."

"Why is that, Lil Kitty?" I asked, not ready to hear what she was about to say.

"Because some nigga named Trigger keeps calling me from Punkin's phone."

"Okay, what does that have to do with me and the Hot Girls?"

"Because every time this nigga calls me, he's trying to get me up there. When deep down in my soul, I know that something foul—very foul—happened to Punkin!"

Now it sounded as if she was heated. "Okay, and your point?"

"Chyna just told me that the last person she saw him with was your special girl, Mignon."

***

The words Countess uttered to my brother had a lasting effect on him as he stood there motionless, drifting back, thinking. Then mumbling to himself, *"I sure hope that won't be me and my brother up there swinging from the same chain."*

Just as he mumbled his sentiments, he saw me and himself swinging opposite of each other—me looking over at him, then spitting out my last words. *"This shit is all your fucking fault. If your selfish ass wouldn't have ever signed that deal with the devil, our asses wouldn't be up here about to be eaten by wild, massive hogs!"*

"Firstborn, yo, Firstborn!" Twan's voice snapped him back to reality. He looked like a lunatic as he turned to Twan with sweat pouring from his wide-ass forehead.

"Yeah, what is it?" he asked, his face now holding a frown.

"Are you alright? You looked like you had left us there for a minute."

"I'm good, why, what's up?" he asked with the weirdest expression he had ever had on his face.

"Nothing—look!" Twan shouted in terror as Firstborn and Fabian looked to their right and saw a slender woman and four kids being brought to the center of the stank-ass corral.

"Who in the hell are they, and why are they being placed inside of the corral? I thought he was going to feed the man to the hogs?" Firstborn voiced, wiping away the sweat drenching his shirt straight through to his jacket.

Then, as if Pierre could read their minds, he turned to the men along with his daughter and said, "He didn't want to talk, fearing that whoever he worked for would kill his family. So I did him one better—I found his family. Now they will all die together. Only difference is, he'll get to witness their deaths before he dies!"

Chapter 24
Cruel Way to Die!

When the battered man saw his loving family right before his bleeding eyes, he frantically screamed out, *"No, Señor Pierre! I will tell you everything you desire to know. Please, just spare my family! Kill me—only me—I beg of you!"*

Pierre looked up at the man with a wicked smirk, then back over at Firstborn and his men as if he was trying to either impress them or put fear in their hearts.

"I'm afraid I can't grant you that wish, my friend. You see, my son probably begged for his life as well before whoever you worked for killed him. So I have to pay a favor for a favor. Now sit back and watch as your family suffers for only a few seconds—not like my son, who suffered far more!"

"Noooooo!" the man screamed as a young girl was tossed into the pit.

Two huge black hogs roared out of the gate, charging directly at the child. She yelled and tried her best to run, but there was one slight problem—her head was covered with a black hood. She couldn't see where she was going and ran right into another massive hog coming from a different direction.

Her precious, tear-jerking screams of torture reached a high only the ears of a crazed and deranged person would want to hear. Within seconds, the three hogs ate the poor girl as if she were just a small snack in dire need of another.

As the first hog tore into her, Twan swiftly turned his head, not wanting to witness such a hideous act, then threw up what he had eaten on the yacht. Countess stood next to Firstborn, smiling deviously at what she had already seen a million times before.

"I guess ole boy can't hold his food, huh?" she asked, looking at Fabian, who was only seconds away from doing the same as Twan.

Just as the second hog wrapped his huge mouth around the girl's neck, he ripped her head clean off her body, chewing on it as if it was the best thing he'd ever eaten.

"Damn, do we have to stand here and watch this appalling act?" Fabian said out loud.

Pierre quickly turned in their direction and shouted, "Why of course, young man! This is what someone receives when they cross me and my family—not to mention when they help the people who killed my son! Now throw the entire family inside the pit at once!"

Twan was still throwing up, Fabian too, while my brother just stood there watching, taking in everything. He told me later he was making sure he didn't show any signs of weakness.

"Are you okay?" Countess asked as she placed her hand on his shoulder.

"I couldn't be better. I'm fine, why do you ask?" he calmly returned.

"Oh, nothing. Just wondering, since your partners over there seem to have weak stomachs." She smirked wickedly.

"I see," he voiced, but deep down he was having second thoughts about agreeing to sell Pierre's cocaine.

While he stood there with those thoughts, one of the housemaids ran out to Pierre with his phone in hand. She told him his people had been found…

***

Back in Tallahassee, the young lady Firstborn had slid his number to was just getting home. She looked at it and decided to give him a call. His phone rang four times before the voicemail clicked on.

"Hello, and thanks for calling. Either I'm on another call or I just can't get to you at this present moment. Please leave your number and a brief message, and I'll get back to you as soon as possible."

The beep followed.

She hesitated, then decided to leave a message. *"Hello, my name is Symone. You met me at the airport earlier today. You can reach me back at 850-242-4563. Thanks, and I'll talk to you then. Peace."*

Symone hung up with anticipation of when she'd meet Firstborn again. The only problem was, if he only knew who he just invited into his business with Pierre Santiago, he might have thought twice about his drastic mistake. Let's just say, this was only the beginning of the end for one of them...

***

Just after getting off the phone with Lil Kitty, I looked down at my watch—it was five fifteen.

"You 'bout ready to go?" I asked.

She cut her eyes at me while sipping on her McDonald's strawberry milkshake. "Yes, sir."

"Okay, go ahead and grab your things."

We both had our hands full with shopping bags. She looked at me, still talking and trying to balance herself.

"Wow, Dad, I don't even get this much stuff at Christmas time."

"Well, this Christmas you should get triple of what you didn't get last year."

"For real?" she asked, excitement written all over her bright young face.

"Yes, my dear. Now let me have your bags so I can place them in the back seat."

"Thank you," she uttered, going to her side of the car and trying to open her door.

"No, hold on, young lady," I shouted before she opened it. "A man should always open the door for a lady. Always remember that."

She looked up at me as she positioned her small body in the seat. "Thank you," she softly whispered as I closed the door.

"What a sweet child I brought into the world," I muttered as I ran around to the driver's side...

Chapter 25
Big Zo!

Big Zo was a big Haitian cat from down south—Miami, FL to be exact. Him and his family resided in Lil Haiti. He wasn't called Big Zo for his large size in nature. He was called Big Zo because of the large number of bricks he could move in a small amount of time. The drugs him and his crew of Vagabonds specialized in were cocaine and heroin.

On this day, him and a few of his men just so happened to be up in Orlando. There was a small amount of business that needed to be dealt with, so he figured it would be best for them to head up to the city.

The same day that old Marc Dawg decided to take Orlando's finest on a high-speed chase in and out of traffic. Right about now he was about to take them through the city neighborhoods. Not caring if he killed someone in the wake of his tortuous driving. All he cared about at that moment was getting away—because if he didn't, he was going to get charged not only with fleeing from the law, but worse, for the two bodies that he had in the trunk of the car.

"Fuck! Why didn't I do what the fuck I was supposed to do?" he shouted, making a quick right onto Silver Star Road.

Big Zo stood six feet even and weighed around two hundred forty-five pounds. Solid brother who worked out religiously every day. He did this so whenever his gangsta was tried, he could handle it well with his hands. He had the skin complexion of a dark chocolate Hershey bar, with long locks that hung down to the small of his back.

He was just about to head over to the mall when he got the frantic call that would put things in motion. His phone rang twice before he answered. The only reason he even picked up was because of the epiphany he had while taking a mean shit thirty minutes earlier. He answered the phone just as he was about to step out the door.

"What it do, playa?" he asked.

"Yo Zo, you still up here in the city?" a frantic voice asked, fear laced in his tone. Marc Dawg knew Zo was in town because both of them were at Cleo's the night before. Cleo's was the strip club where Marc Dawg linked up with the two strippers from.

"Yeah, Marc, why you ask, my man?" Zo replied, just as a few of his men ran inside yelling about police cars and a helicopter.

"Listen up, man, I can't really talk right now!" Marc shouted into his phone.

Zo tried making sense of what Marc was going through, but was suddenly interrupted by one of his men.

"Yo Zo, look at this shit, my nigga!" Haitian Fred shouted, pointing at the television. On the screen was the police chase the local news was reporting on.

"I'm 'bout to drive this piece-of-shit car into the same apartments you're at right now—Mercy Drive!"

"Hold on, playa, you're not driving a raggedy ass Bonneville right now, are you?" Zo asked, eyes glued to the screen.

"Yes, that I am!"

"Nigga, you got what looks like the entire Orlando police department on your ass!" Zo told him.

"And don't forget one fucking helicopter!" Haitian Fred shouted, still glued to the TV.

"Yeah, Marc, what about the helicopter that's on your ass?" Zo asked with concern.

"I know, my man. Just you and your people be ready for my black ass when I pull into the parking lot."

"I got that part, Marc, but what is it that you want me and my men to do?" Zo asked curiously.

"Zo, you niggas know what to do! As soon as I zip into that bitch, you niggas start laying down some cover fire for me."

"What?" Zo asked, thinking he misheard.

"You heard me, my nigga! When I pull into that parking lot, you niggas start blasting. Make sure you shoot up this fucking car."

"Okay, is there anything else?"

"Yeah, make sure you guys shoot at the trunk, so this piece-of-shit car can explode!"

"Explode? Why is that? Isn't there work inside the trunk?" Zo asked, confused.

"Nah, my nigga. But if I get caught with what's in this trunk, I might not never see daylight again!"

"What in the hell do you have in the trunk, silly ass nigga?"

"Try two dead niggas from North Carolina!" Marc said.

"Oh Lord, this nigga done lost his rabbit ass mind!" Zo shouted, just as Marc Dawg pulled onto Mercy Drive after making a left off Silver Star Road. The brother turned the corner doing at least eighty. One could say he should have been a NASCAR driver instead of a drug dealer on the run...

***

Just a few miles away, across town, Mo Money was waking up from her beauty sleep. It was about time to start getting ready for the show. The first thing that came to mind was the fact she hadn't heard from her silly ass brother yet.

"What time is it?" she asked herself, stretching and yawning as she searched for the remote. She turned on the TV.

It was a little past five in the evening. "Okay, just enough time for me to grab a bite to eat, then jump in the shower," she mumbled, reaching for her phone to call me, to see what time I'd be through to pick her up. But when she saw what was transpiring on the screen, her heart dropped straight out of her chest.

"Damn you, Marc Dawg!" she shouted. She didn't know if he had done what he was told. Falling back onto her bed, it dawned on her there was no way in hell he had. If he would have, the police wouldn't be chasing him in the same car she told him to destroy—right along with the two dead niggas she had murdered...

***

When Marc Dawg never came back with the food or their money, both females knew they'd been screwed over. They'd been with the young man all morning, him fucking the shit out of both of them. Now here they were with no ride back to their spot, so they decided to pay for another night. From there, they'd make their way back down to Cleo's where they danced.

"So, do you want to grab something to eat since ole boy stood us up?" the slim female asked her friend.

The redbone Marc Dawg really wanted stood in the mirror doing her hair. "Yeah, why not? So what did ole boy say before he left?" Marsha asked her slim friend, Candance.

"The nigga said he was coming right back with our food and money. But that was about three hours ago," Candance spat, sitting on the edge of the bed when something on the TV caught her eye.

"Well I guess we both gave up some pussy without getting paid. Why didn't you wake me up? At least I could've went with the nigga, so he could've came back with our money?" Marsha asked, walking out of the bathroom.

When Candance didn't answer right away, she pressed her. "Candance, I know you hear me talking to you?"

"Shh! I think I know why ole boy never came back! Look!" was all she said, pointing at the screen.

Right there in front of them was the car chase Marc Dawg was involved in.

"Is that ole boy?" Marsha asked, sitting down on her goldmine.

Marsha Amber Jenkins was her name. She stood five-foot-six, weighed about one thirty-five. Real high yellow female with a banging body. Ass round like a honeydew melon, ripe to be exact. On her chest she carried two perfect breasts, at least 36C. The female was hands down gorgeous. Cute pearly whites you couldn't miss when she flashed her amazing smile.

Now her friend Candance Berneice Williams wasn't blessed with the looks or frame of her best friend. She stood five-foot-four, weighed about ninety-five pounds soaking wet. No titties, no ass. The only reason the club even let her dance was because Marsha was too scared to dance without her. Plus, Baby Lack told the club to give her a break, so they did.

"Yes, girl, that is his ass," Candance mumbled.

"How you know?" Marsha asked, her heart racing for Marc Dawg. Not only was her heart racing, but her pussy and ass throbbed from the fucking he had put on her fine ass.

"Girl, you don't remember that ugly ass car he had us in this morning?" Candance said, staring her friend down.

"Oh snap! That is that bucket of a car he had us in," Marsha voiced, her mental all over the place.

"Yes it is. And whatever it is his ass is in, I bet you them crackers are gonna offer a reward if he makes it out alive."

She voiced it with dollar signs dancing around her mind. But Marsha had other plans for the young man—plans dancing around inside her head…

Chapter 26
Vivica Fox!

The very first night that Marsha and Candance danced at Cleo's, everyone thought that she was the younger sister to Vivica Fox, since she resembled a younger version of the beautiful actress. Once she told everyone that she wasn't, they all felt that her stage name should be Ms. Fox. And when Baby Lack introduced her as that on her first night, the name stuck like glue. Just like her feelings for Marc Dawg, when he put that dick on her fine red ass. She had fallen for the man the instant his swollen dick head split her walls. To her at that time, she didn't even know that she liked bad boys. Now that she sees the man on the screen, being chased by the cops, she knew that she wanted to be in his life.

"I hope they don't kill him!" Marsha shouted with her hands over her mouth.

Me too, we need that nigga to somehow get away, so that we can collect on that reward money that's going to be on that nigga's head, Candance versed as she sat there on the bed. Her stomach was touching her back by now.

"So what, if his ass gets away, you're going to snitch the man out?" Marsha asked as she stared at her girl.

"You damn right! Fuck that nigga! His ass fucked the both of us and then left us here with no money and no food! Hell, I'm hungrier than a muthafucka!" Lil Candance said as she stood up to walk into the bathroom. Just as she stood up, her lil nasty ass farted. "BURRRRR!" It sounded as Marsha stared at her nasty ass; she curled up her lips and shouted,

"Bitch, take your stank ass in there and handle your business!"

"That's exactly what I'm about to do!"

"And close the door, because you lil ass already stanking!" When the door closed, Marsha reached into her pants pocket and retrieved a piece of paper. To her surprise it was the number to Marc Dawg, with around three hundred dollars with it, right along with a small note.

"Hey you, had a great time this morning. Here is a little something for you, but not for Slim. Along with the skrilla is my name and number, get at me when you're not with yo girl, peace. Marc Dawg!"

The note brought a cute smile onto her lovely face, causing her to look back at the screen. "Your ass better get away, so I can have your babies!"

***

By the time that I had walked around the back of the vehicle, little Mykel was already buckled up, nice and tight, ready to go. I sluggishly sat down in the driver's seat and looked over at her and said, "So what else do we do besides go home?"

"I don't know, it seems like we've done everything already." She replied as she looked up at me, smiling.

"You know, you're absolutely right. Let's go home." I said as I turned the key in the ignition. Just as I made a quick right out of the parking lot, headed toward Highway Fifty—knowing that during that time of the day the O-Cee Mall traffic would be very busy and I definitely wanted to beat the five o'clock traffic headed back through Metro West—I was just about to make small talk with my young child, who really seemed like she knew way too much for her young age. But all hopes of that conversation were exhausted, just as much as she was, as I looked at her: already fast asleep, her small head leaned up against the door of my vehicle.

I guess she had been tired from all the daily activities she had me going through. Not to mention that I had *"Burning 4 You"* by Jon B playing through my sound system, which helped put me in the mood for some much-needed sleep. So I gently leaned over and placed her head back up against her seat, then bent a right at the light when my cell phone rang with Tamika on the other line.

"Hello."

"Hey, Michael, are you there?" The voice snapped me back to reality, causing me to say, "Well hello to you also, young lady." I said before getting to her question.

"I'm so sorry, my bad. How are you doing?" she asked.

"That's more like it." I smirked, then said, "She's doing just fine with her lil grown ass."

"Yes, she can be grown at times. My mother actually believes that she's been here before."

"I can see that. You know, I can believe that too."

"Can I speak with her, please?"

"Yes, you could if she was awake. It seems like she couldn't hang with her dad and fell asleep."

"Already? What was she doing, playing all day?"

"Nah, your lil grown ass daughter talked me into taking her shopping for some school clothes. Talking about she didn't have any over at my house."

"So you took her shopping?"

"Yes—and it seems like she should have enough clothes for the rest of the school year and probably a few years after that."

"Well I guess she's a lot smarter than I took her for."

"Why do you say that?" I asked as I made a left turn at the light, headed down Kirkman Road.

"Because, Mr. Michael, she's coming home, so why would she need school clothes over there?"

I cut my eye over at the little swindler who was fast asleep. "Yeah, I guess I got played."

"Oh well, it doesn't hurt for her to have more clothes. I just hope that you're not spoiling her."

"It's too late for that, she's adorable. My heart was taken by her the minute I laid eyes on her."

"Well thank you, she gets all that from her gorgeous mother."

"Whatever, she might get a few good looks from you, but the rest she gets from her father." I told her, then she hit me with something I had forgotten all about.

"Well Michael, I have no problem with her being with you and all, but what are you going to tell your beloved Sharon?" *Oh shit, I hadn't even spoken to Sharon all day.* I thought to myself. Then I said, "That's a good question. I guess either she's going to have to learn to deal with it or else simply move on."

"Whatever Michael, you know as well as I know that you're not going to settle down without Sharon in your complicated life." Then, just as if she knew that we were talking about her, my phone beeped; letting me know that I had another call coming through.

I pulled my phone down from my ear to see who was calling. "Speaking of Sharon, that's her beeping in on my other line. I'm going to have to call you back."

"I understand, playa. Call me as soon as my little Rag-A-Muffin wakes up."

"Will do, Tamika. Peace." I quickly uttered, just as I clicked over and said, "Hello, Pumpkin."

"Don't hello me, Pumpkin, when your black ass hasn't called me all day!" She sounded—she sounded pissed, but when has she not been pissed at my ass?

Chapter 27
Before Sunset!

All hopes for their rescue looked great at the time. But miles away the Coast Guard got word of some people being rescued out in the Atlantic Ocean. Once they received word, Lt. William Barney of the Coast Guard made a quick phone call. The phone rang twice before the person on the other line answered.

"Agent Tony Vazquez, this is Lt. William Barney with the South Carolina Coast Guard. Are you busy right now?" the highly decorated Coast Guard officer asked.

"No, not at all," he replied, then said, "Please tell me that you guys have the individuals from the plane we were tailing?" Agent Vazquez asked with optimism. His pulse raced as he waited for his answer.

"Not quite yet, but we just got word that some individuals from that plane have been rescued. Some of my men are on the way to bring them in for questioning as we speak."

"Great, my partner and I are on our way to South Carolina right now," Agent Vazquez versed as he went for his sport coat and pointed over at his partner, alerting him of the news.

"No problem, Agent. We'll make sure to hold them until you guys arrive here in beautiful South Carolina."

"Sounds like a plan," the eager-sounding agent said, triumphantly. The night the Jacksonville Police Department had received information of Pierre's plane being at the airport, the police department also got a tip that the plane might be carrying drugs on board. This was just the news they wanted to hear, ever since that night when the plane they were chasing decided to fly over the Bermuda Triangle rather than turn around so the plane could be searched. To the police department, the plane deciding to do this instead of turning around meant one thing and one thing only…

***

The small fishing boat that had just rescued the crew of the plane was just about to pull away from the island when Miguel told the owner of the boat, "Please wait a few minutes more, please! There's still one more person left somewhere around here!" he emphatically told the men.

"Yes, my sister has to be around here somewhere! Did you all spot any signs of anyone on the way here?" Natasha asked in sheer panic, her emotions all over the place as she stared the owner of the boat in his eyes.

"No, not any signs of anyone, but we did run into a few sharks, who seemed to be eating what looked like a large shark that had been killed by something or someone!" When the man's words left his mouth, Miguel's heart dropped directly out of his chest.

"What was that?" Maria interrupted.

"Yes, it was the strangest thing I have ever seen. In my entire life of fishing these waters, I have never seen sharks feasting on another one in the manner in which they were," Dwight Spears said to the people he and his only son had just rescued.

"Really?" Natasha asked with a bit of hope in her voice.

"Yes." Dwight said, then continued, "If there is someone else still missing from your crew, maybe the Coast Guard has already saved them."

"Oh no! We can't have that! Does the Coast Guard know that you have us on board your fishing boat?" Natasha asked with an intensified look on her face.

"I'm not quite sure, but I did tell them that me and my son would be on the lookout for any survivors of the crash."

"What did they say?" Natasha asked as he began looking around.

"To call them immediately if we found anyone!" his young son answered, sweat pouring down his young face.

"We can't have that. Let me have your phones now, please! I have to make a call."

"But why do you need both of our phones?" the son asked as he went into his pocket to retrieve his phone.

"Let's just say that the people who you guys have just rescued are some very important people. And if we fall into the wrong hands, our lives could be over."

"There's no need to worry, your safety and identities are safe with us," Dwight spoke.

"We can't take that chance. Now please render me your phones." Natasha asked as she held her hand out...

***

Firstborn was scared shit-less; he just couldn't show it as he stood tall, watching the last hog chew and devour the last family member of the man hanging from the chain. His stomach didn't know if it wanted to spit up the food he had eaten as well, when Pierre yelled out to the man.

"Now do you want to tell me everything it is that I desire to know?" The man hung from the chain as if he was in another place—twitching, shaking, convulsing—trying to erase the horrible memories of his helpless family being eaten by the wild boars.

"Manny Alvarez, do you hear me?" Pierre barked, poking at the deterring man, hoping that the man would say something that could help him and his men in finding who was responsible for the death of his son.

"Damn," Firstborn whispered as he gazed up at the man, then looked over at his two goons, who he thought were two hungry young men he could trust. "Hey, I hope you two are through throwing up all of your guts. Now wipe your mouths and pull yourselves together!"

"Whatever, man, you never said anything about us having to watch an entire family being eaten by some got-damn pigs!" Twan yelled as he stayed bent over with his hands on his knees.

"Wait a minute, don't tell me that you have some weaklings working for you, Mr. Valentino?" Pierre asked as he turned to look at Firstborn.

"Hell nah, my brother just has a very weak stomach, that's all," Fabian yelled as he came to the rescue of his younger brother, patting him on his back and giving him something to wipe his mouth with.

"I see," Pierre voiced as he turned back to the man, still jerking and twitching as he hung from the chain.

"Now back to you. Are you ready to talk?" The man slowly pulled his head up from where it hung in his chest, then looked as if he was possessed, with red eyes that cut straight through Firstborn's soul, causing my brother to flinch as their eyes met.

This is when the man began to rant, yelling in what sounded like broken English and Spanish. "I can tell you one thing, Señor Pierre Santiago: the people responsible for your son's death and yours will surely come sooner than you think! They closer to you than you think! We have people all around you! We can touch you any time we see fit! Fuck you, puta!" the man shouted with saliva spraying wildly as he shouted out in anger. Then, quickly and without hesitation, Pierre snatched the firearm that was held tightly by one of his men and pointed at the man hanging.

Blam-blam! Two shots rang out as the first bullet split dead-center mass of his face. Blood and brain matter flew everywhere. The second bullet caved into his chest cavity just as Pierre shouted, "Fuck 'em! Now let the hogs eat the rest of his shitty ass body! When you are done, find his entire family. I want his entire bloodline dead before sunset!" Pierre then looked at Firstborn and shouted, "Now back to our business at hand. Follow me, while my men take care of that awful mess!" he said, referring to the dead corpse hanging from the chain.

"Yo, you think we're ready for this type of lifestyle?"

"I don't know, but it's probably too late to change our minds now, baby brother," Fabian told his brother as they turned to walk behind Firstborn and Pierre...

Chapter 28
The Godfather!

Pierre placed his hand on Firstborn's shoulder, ushering him and his two goons away from the hideous sight of the dead man slowly swinging from the beam. Then, turning to Firstborn with a wicked smirk, he asked the dreaded question.

"So how much more of my product do you need to take back with you?"

Damn! he thought, really not wanting to take any of the man's precious product. All due to the fear of becoming just like what his eyes had just witnessed. But it was too late for that—he had already crossed the line. He couldn't let Pierre know of his fear, so he said,

"Business is very good where I am, and now that I've enlisted the help of my two friends here, I think that maybe I should be upgrading to a much larger quantity of your fine product."

Pierre smiled. It was music to his ears, hearing Firstborn boast about business and more product.

"Well, in that case, gentlemen, please follow me." He said to all three men, while Twan looked over at Fabian and whispered, "What the fuck did his ass just tell the man?"

"More product," Fabian replied, shaking his head in disbelief, rethinking their decision to help Firstborn sell Pierre's product—a decision that just might cost one of the three their life.

"Has that nigga lost his rabbit ass mind? Man, I am not about to be hanging from a gotdamn chain, waiting on some wild boars to eat my black ass!" Twan voiced in anger.

"I feel you, just be cool. I might know somebody that can push a lot of the work his ass is about to get." Fabian smiled, thinking of his good friend from Gainesville, FL, who not only pushed mad quantities of heroin, but sometimes indulged in that white girl (cocaine) also.

"Who?" Twan asked.

Fabian cut a half grin at his brother. "You remember that smooth ass brutha from Gainesville named Junior?"

"Talking about the brown-skinned, heavy-set dude with the short dreadlocks?"

"Yes."

"Oh yeah, the dude with the kid brother whose name was Josh?"

"Yeah, son, them two. That's who I know we can get off a few bricks to."

"But I thought the kid Josh was from Georgia?"

"He is, but where the nigga lives has nothing to do with us moving this product."

"Say less then." Twan smiled.

"You damn right. We can sell that nigga two birds for the price of one kilo of heroin."

You see, Junior and Josh were brothers who had the same mother but different fathers. Junior lived in Gainesville, while his little brother Joshua Smalls lived somewhere in Georgia. Both of them were paying around sixty thousand a key for heroin. Fabian figured—why not have them purchase two birds of cocaine for that price?

Twan's face lit up like a Christmas tree, thinking of all the money him and his brother would be making between themselves.

"And to make the deal even better, we're going to give them a really good price so they won't refuse our offer."

"Listen to your ass." Twan grinned at his brother.

"What, baby brother?"

"You think you're the Godfather now, huh?"

"Why you say that?" Fabian asked, laughing as he walked behind Firstborn and Pierre.

"Because nigga, Marlon Brando said the same thing in the movie *The Godfather*. That's why, ole silly ass nigga."

Fabian liked the name. He liked it so well, he had to say it loud a few times.

"Yeah, just like the Godfather, my young brother."

While the two of them talked amongst themselves, they didn't realize they were standing at the entrance of the huge building that housed all the cocaine and the naked people who worked inside. Pierre stood at the entrance, staring at the men.

"What you men are about to witness, only a few gentlemen have had the pleasure of seeing. So please be mindful of what your eyes are about to behold."

As he slowly opened the door, their eyes enlarged at the sight before them.

"My God, is all of this yours?" a dumbfounded Fabian asked in astonishment.

"Why, of course it is, young man. What was your name again?" Pierre asked, as if making a mental note.

"Fabian, sir," he replied, his eyes still trying to focus on the large quantity of pure cocaine.

Meanwhile, Twan had his eyes on all the fine, butt-naked Spanish women. Every one of them had nice bodies, along with cute ass faces. Not one of them looked a day over thirty.

After calming Ms. Sharon down, she wanted to know if it was okay for her to come over later with some dinner from Red Lobster. At that moment, my face turned into a full frown as I had to tell her,

"That sounds nice and all, Sharon, but we have a show tonight in Gainesville."

She quickly came back at me, sounding all dejected and shit.

"But I thought that you guys didn't dance anymore since Lil Kitty caused you all to lose the Caribbean Beach Night Club?"

I could hear disappointment all in her voice. At this point and juncture of my life, how I wish I would have made better choices—maybe things would have played out much better between me and Ms. Sharon.

"That's correct, my dear, but it seems as though there's a new rap group emerging on the scene, and the venue has them performing there tonight."

She quickly interjected,

"And let me guess, they want your girls there for the extra entertainment, right?"

"Yes, that they do. And besides, the money they're paying me to bring the Hot Girls is a pretty penny."

"Whatever, Mike?" she said, sucking her lips.

"What, please don't tell me that you're a slight bit jealous of the Hot Girls?"

"Hell nah! Why would I be? Ain't none of them females as bad as Ms. Sharon is! That's why I be having your black ass foaming all over these goods. Close your mouth—you probably want to suck out this pussy right now, don't cha?"

I quickly looked over at my little angel in the front seat, then said,

"Yeah, right, Sharon."

"See, I knew you did. Now do you want me to bring this pussy over so you can taste it?"

"Tomorrow, when I wake up from tonight's show," I told her, trying my best not to wake up my princess.

"Bye, Michael," she said, then hung up. I guess she didn't like my answer.

After I hung up, I was pulling into my driveway. I still needed to get inside and prepare for the show and the ride up to Gainesville. Gainesville, FL was about an hour and a half from Orlando. So I had just enough time to get ready and find out who would be babysitting my little angel.

I was so preoccupied with my daughter that I never noticed the small piece of car that was in my yard. But I was surely about to have my memory jogged once I walked inside my house. I was about to see someone I hadn't seen for quite some time.

Boy, how times had changed…

Chapter 29
Mrs. Camisha Vallentino!

My day had been a very long one. From earlier in the morning having sex with the flawless-looking Mignon, to spending my entire afternoon with my newfound angel, all I needed now was to be told about my houseguest, who I had no idea even knew where I resided.

Just as I made it to my front door, I was greeted by Nicole and Mignon. Both were wearing their outfits for tonight's show.

"Well damn, don't you two look nice?" I asked, standing there with Mykel in my arms.

"Why thank you, sir," they both spoke in unison.

"And who's the little one in your arms?" Nicole asked as she leaned forward and placed a kiss on my lips.

"It's my daughter," I uttered.

"Daughter? Well, I know she can't be the daughter of the woman who's inside your foyer waiting on your arrival." Mignon spoke, while Nicole was still smitten by the young one in my outstretched arms.

"What are you rambling about, Mignon?" I asked, pushing past Nicole.

"In there. There's a woman here who says that she's your wife," Mignon told me as I stared at her.

I must admit, both her and Nicole looked inviting in their outfits as they stood there. They looked so inviting that a part of me wanted to take both of them right there in the doorway of my home. But then there was the presence of a woman claiming to be my wife.

There was no way in hell it would be Carrie Lou. She was my first wife, the only one I could think of at the moment. That was until I heard her voice. How could I have forgotten about her—she was the one who had pushed me right into the arms of The Florida Hot Girls.

"Hello Michael. What, you don't know me anymore?" she asked, standing in my foyer looking just as beautiful as the first night I met her at Club Amvets.

"Camisha, what are you doing here, and how did you find me?" I asked, still holding Mykel, while Mignon and Nicole stood at my side.

"Whose child do you have there, Michael?" she asked, almost sounding as if the sight hurt her.

"It's my daughter."

"Which one, Kina or Aerial?" she asked, walking closer. Both females moved in tighter toward me. For a brief moment, I thought they were about to go into attack mode. So I stepped in and said, "Neither one of them. It seems as though I had another daughter when I lived here. I just found out a few weeks ago."

"I see. She's cute." Camisha forced the words out, though I knew she didn't want to.

"Ladies, if you two don't mind, could you please take her up to her room?"

"Sure thing, Mike. Are you going to be okay?"

"He'll be just fine, young ladies," Camisha cut in, looking at them, then back at me. Her eyes had the look of an animal as she stood there. I could sense she had something on her mind.

"So, what do I owe the pleasure of you finding me and just popping up?"

"Let me cut straight to the chase, Michael. I'm miserable without you home with me and the kids. So, in other words, you need to come back home."

She might as well have punched me in the gut. She even had the nerve to smile as she said it.

"Come back home?" I asked curiously. "And leave all of this?"

"Yes, Michael. Life hasn't been the same since you've been gone. I can't sleep nor eat without you," she told me. I just sat there, reminiscing about how bad this woman had treated me in the past. And now to hear her ask me to come back home with her and her bad-ass kids?

"I'm really sorry to hear that, Camisha. But as you can see, I'm doing quite well for myself. And the question you're asking me right now would actually be a frivolous move on my part."

I stood and walked to my window, needing to look away from her. Even though I hadn't seen her in a while, she still looked gorgeous—still had the body of a goddess.

There was a pause in our conversation. I turned around to see what she was doing. Her face looked confused as she asked, "What does frivolous mean?"

"It means not having any serious purpose or value," I explained.

"So you're saying moving back home with me and the kids would make no sense?"

"Basically," I answered quickly.

"So you would rather be here inside this big-ass house, surrounded by nothing but butt-naked hoes?" A single tear tried to escape the bottom of her right eye as she stared at me.

"Hell yeah. Shiiit, when I lived with you, you didn't even want to sleep with me or make love to me," I told her, staring directly into her eyes.

"That's all because of the starch I be eating. But I'm not eating it anymore."

From the first day I met her, she liked eating corn starch straight out of the box. She'd even stick a straw in it and suck it out. When I asked what it tasted like, she told me it tasted like whatever she desired. One day she said it tasted like ice cream. I would later find out many females in the projects liked eating corn starch. That's where Camisha lived most of her younger adult life, but you couldn't tell by the way she carried herself.

"Oh yeah? So when did you stop?"

"Does it matter? You still don't want to come back home."

"No, ma'am. I tried to be a happily married man, but you and those kids changed all that. Matter of fact, one could say y'all shitted all over those dreams."

"Michael, I've changed, seriously!" she cried.

As I sat gazing at her, a part of me tried to sympathize, but in the back of my mind, I could hear my probation officer's voice, when he told me Camisha might be suffering from a chemical imbalance.

"Do you hear me talking to you?" she snapped, pulling me back to reality.

"Yeah, I hear you. But I believe you might have a slight chemical imbalance."

"So you trying to say I'm crazy or something, Michael?"

Now I had really struck a nerve. Before she lashed out at me with those paws of hers, I quickly came back with, "I didn't say that."

Just as I said it, the door to my home flew wide open.

"What the fuck?" I shouted as I stood. And you're not gonna believe who burst through my front door.

"Camisha, if his ass hasn't packed his shit yet, his ass is not coming back home with us! Now come on, you promised me some McDonald's!"

Her short-ass son Taz shouted while I stood there with my mouth wide open.

"Taz, I'm coming! Now get back to the car!" she yelled at Lil Man, who in turn said, "Don't worry, I got the keys right here. If you're not outside before I get to the car, me and Shayla are gone!"

"Damn, the lil' nigga can talk and drive?" I asked her as she turned back around.

"No, you know he's too short to see over the steering wheel."

"I heard that!" he shouted, slamming my front door.

"Now you see why I will not ever come back to that house."

"Why, because of my kids?" she asked like that was the problem.

"No, Camisha. It's just us. There's no way we could ever make it," I told her as gently as I could without crushing her feelings.

But truth be told, there was a part of me that really wanted to be with Camisha. Then there was the other part of me—The Florida Hot Girls had full control over that...

***

Firstborn stood smiling at the brothers' reaction, secretly hiding his fear of the man next to him. He finally realized Pierre cared only for his product and family. So without thinking of his own family—or the risk he was putting everyone in—Firstborn simply uttered,

"Let me have around two hundred of them thangs."

"What?" Fabian yelled as he turned to Firstborn, then slowly turned to Pierre, who was standing there all smiles.

"Be cool, my brother. Trust me, I know what I'm doing," Firstborn recited, placing his hand on Fabian's shoulder and pulling him closer.

"Wait a minute, Smooth. Have you thought this shit out?" Twan asked.

"Twan, when I say trust me, that's exactly what the fuck I mean! Now be quiet and trust me."

Firstborn then turned back to Pierre and said, "Are you good with the number I so dreadfully need?"

Deep down he was hoping and praying Pierre wouldn't agree to such a large quantity of product.

"Ahhh, Señor, are you sure you can handle that much product?" Pierre asked, his two devilish horns beginning to show.

"Yes, sir. Just as long as one of your planes takes us back, I should have no problem dealing with that much product."

"Alright, well, I shall have my men load up the product while we go inside and work out some numbers."

"Damn," Firstborn mumbled under his breath.

"Are you guys hungry?" Pierre asked. "With the large quantity of product you all want, it has made me a very hungry man."

He waved at the naked ladies, then barked, "Have Rico and Chavez load up two hundred kilos immediately!"

"Yes, Señor! Will there be anything else?"

"That will be all." He looked back at the three men. "Follow me, I shall have more places set at the table."

The men started walking back toward the house, when the thought of the hogs eating the family crossed Twan's mind. He abruptly stopped and shouted,

"Excuse me, sir, you don't have a problem with me skipping dinner, do you?"

Pierre briskly turned around in stride and replied, "What's wrong, you're not hungry?"

"Nah, it's not that. It's just the thought of those people being ate by them fucking pigs!"

"Nonsense, young man. Don't let the sight of a few people being eaten by wild hogs hinder your appetite."

"Yes, sir," Twan said.

"Why, if you think that was bad, wait until it's you and your brother being up there, watching your mother JoAnn and your sister Deidra being eaten by those same hogs."

"What the fuck did you just say about our mother and sister?" Fabian shouted …

124

Chapter 30
Family First!

Pierre was just a few steps ahead of the men when he stopped and turned around. A sinister grin covered his face as he said, "Excuse me?"

Fabian had fire in his eyes, almost reaching for his piece. "You said something about my family. Something about them being eaten by pigs, just like that family who just got ate."

"No the fuck he didn't, Fabian! Nigga, you trippin'. Shut the fuck up!" Firstborn shouted as he stared the young man down.

"Didn't you hear him, Twan?" Fabian asked, confusion on his face.

"Nah, son. He was saying something totally different," Twan told him.

"Damn, my ass really trippin'," Fabian muttered to himself as Pierre turned on his heels. He was just about to enter the large dining room when he turned to Firstborn.

"Your associate's nerves are already beginning to fuck with him. You sure he's cut out for this line of work?"

"My man is solid," Firstborn told him. But truthfully, Pierre should've been worried about my foolish brother. He had just bit off more than he could chew—putting not only his life on the line but many others, as you'll find out later down the road.

Once they arrived at the entrance, one of the maids opened the door and bowed her head when Pierre entered.

"I hope that whatever we're having for dinner, you and your friends find it to your enjoyment."

"Whatever it is, it sure as hell smells good," Firstborn sputtered as he caught Countess standing off to the side of the kitchen, chewing on a carrot. When their eyes met, he nodded his head. She did the same, watching him like a hawk, while he and his men observed the spread laid out before them.

It was a stunning sight, like a Thanksgiving dinner. This was when Twan and Fabian met the rest of the family as they took their seats at the table—eager, ready to eat, and then get back home. The food smelled delicious as they finished saying grace.

"Well, I guess I can nibble on a lil' something, since it'd be rude not to eat," Twan whispered to his brother.

"Exactly. It shouldn't be that bad. Hell, it smells good," Fabian replied, ready to dig in.

"I guess, just as long as we're not having—" Twan's voice trailed off when he saw the dish laid out ahead of him. Fabian's eyes damn near popped out his head when he saw the entrée too.

Twan's mouth dropped as his head fell onto his brother's shoulder.

"No! These sons of bitches ain't trying to serve us some gotdamn pig? We just had to stand and watch them pigs out back eat an entire family! Now we about to eat the damn pig?"

Twan was furious, about to stand up and excuse himself.

"No, silly. This is not the pigs from out back. These pigs are from the market, so you have nothing to fear," Countess uttered as she looked over to Firstborn and told him to pass the gravy.

"Sure," he replied, though he too was shocked at the choice of meal, stuffing his mouth with hot buttered biscuits …

***

Just as Marc Dawg whipped into the project's parking lot, he slowed and did the unthinkable. The driver-side door flew open as he leapt from the seat. The car kept rolling toward the statue in the middle of the courtyard. At least five police cars were behind it when he jumped out.

Kids had been playing, folks were barbecuing outside their apartments. But when the gunshots rang out, everybody scattered like German cockroaches. No hesitation. Some might've thought it was firecrackers—but not the good folks of these projects.

Between the screaming, yelling, and sheer terror came the thunder of gunfire.

BLAM! BLAM! BLAM! RAT-TAT-TAT-TAT!

It sounded like a 12-gauge blast mixed with AR-15s and Glocks. Rounds popped off nonstop while the cops ducked for cover. Bullets came from everywhere. The police hesitated to shoot back, not wanting to hit someone's apartment and kill an innocent bystander.

"Make sure not to hit any bystander!" Big Zo shouted instructions as he and his men fired at the cruisers.

Meanwhile, Marc Dawg stayed ducked off in an empty apartment.

"Yo Fred!" Big Zo shouted.

"Yeah, man!" he answered back.

"Make sure someone hits the car's gas tank!"

"Got it!" Fred shouted, then yelled to his brothers and cousins, "Blow that piece of shit car the fuck up!"

Two minutes later the car exploded.

BOOOOOOOOOM!

The blast triggered car alarms while the cops stood in shock.

"I want everyone involved with this hideous crime arrested by sunset!" the lead officer shouted as his team scrambled around the complex …

Chapter 31
The Aftermath!

Back at the hotel, Marsha and Candance were glued to the TV. Neither could believe what they'd just seen. The room stayed silent until Stank broke it.

"Oh boy must got somebody prayin' for his ass, the way he just got away and shit!"

"I know that's right. I just hope them crackers don't find his ass, 'cause if they do, they gone kill 'em!" Marsha said, standing to get a drink.

Her back was turned when she heard the words that nearly made her fly across the dirty hotel room.

"No problem—they ain't gone kill him. I'm 'bout to call them crackers and let them know who the fuck his ass is!"

Marsha's head whipped around like it was on a swivel.

"Damn, bitch! You a snitch for real!" she screamed, leaping across the bed and slapping the phone out of Candance's hand.

"Don't do that! So you just gone help them crackers lock his ass up, huh?"

"You gotdamn right! Must I remind your pretty ass—that nigga had both of us screamin' at the top of our lungs with all that dick he was fuckin' us with! Then he had the nerve to fuck you in the ass and shove his long dick down my throat! Didn't even wipe his shit off first!"

"Damn, that's why your breath smelled like ass," Marsha laughed hard at her friend.

"That shit ain't funny, bitch! That's probably why I been back and forth to the bathroom all day."

"Why?"

"Think about it, hoe. His dick probably had some shit on it that got in my stomach. Got me round here with the bubble guts and shit!"

"Well listen, that still ain't no reason for you to call them people on the man."

"It ain't about him—it's for the reward money!"

"Bitch, please. Once your black ass tells, they not giving you jack shit! Now come on, we gotta get ready for the club."

Marsha told her, though deep down she knew she couldn't trust her …

***

Mo. Money couldn't believe what she was seeing on TV as the car with bodies in the trunk went up in flames.

"I hope his ass got out safe," she muttered, grabbing her phone.

"Pick up this phone, Marc!" she said as she dialed.

Meanwhile, Marc Dawg was still hidden away in one of the empty apartments. He wasn't about to let the police catch him. Deep in a bedroom, he listened to the chaos outside— the fire trucks, the neighbors. Just as he peeked around the corner, he heard the faint chatter of a police radio.

"Oh shit," he whispered, spotting a lone officer about to enter. He ducked back, heart pounding.

"If this muthafucka steps inside this apartment, I'm choking the shit out his ass," he mumbled, eyes glued on the cop.

The officer seemed like he might turn back—but then it happened.

Ring-ring!

Marc Dawg's cell phone went off loud as hell.

"What the fuck?" he hissed, snatching it off his hip, praying the officer didn't hear. But he did. His mistake was not calling for backup.

"Hello!" Marc Dawg answered.

"Bro! What the fuck, didn't I tell you to take that—" Mo. Money started before Marc cut her off.

"I fucked up! Now listen, I can't talk!"

"So you made it out before the car blew up?"

"I had to—if I'm talkin' to you, right?"

"I see... so what you gonna do now?"

"Right now, I'm hiding from this officer right outside the door. Now let me get off this phone before his ass finds me!" he whispered.

"Wait, you need me to come get you?"

"Yeah, sounds like a—" Marc started, but stopped when both he and Mo. Money heard it:

"Freeze! Hands where I can see 'em!"

The lone officer had his gun pointed right in Marc's face.

"Damn," Marc muttered under his breath, dropping his phone to the floor.

All hope of escape was gone. Mo. Money fell back on her bed, her young life flashing before her eyes as reality set in ...

Chapter 32
Knockout!

On the other line, one could barely hear her screams.

"Marc Dawg! Marc Dawg!" Mo. Money shouted as her worst nightmare had come into fruition. Her half-brother Marc Dawg had been apprehended, and now she was left to wonder what would become of the man. Not to mention, what would happen if the police found the two dead bodies in the trunk of the smoldering Bonneville.

As tears of dread and misfortune welled in her eyes, she didn't realize she still had the phone to her ear. In the background, she could hear the officer shouting.

"Keep your muthafucking hands where I can see them! Please don't give me probable cause to blow your fucking face off!" the cop recited, keeping his gun aimed at Marc Dawg's nose, then reaching for his cuffs with his other hand.

"Man, don't shoot me! I know how dirty you Orlando cops can be!"

"Shut the fuck up!" the cop uttered. "I'm bound to get a raise and promotion for catching the nigger responsible for all this mess!"

"Wait a minute! I'm not who you're looking for. I'm just here hiding inside this empty apartment!" he lied, trying to convince the officer. Right now he needed a miracle if he wanted to remain a free Black man.

"Yeah, right—and my name is Officer Boo-Boo the Fool!" the cop muttered through gritted teeth.

All the cop could see was that promotion and maybe a giant leap up the food chain. But if only he could've seen what Marc Dawg saw, coming through the open door of the bando. The cop noticed the surprised look on Marc's face and suddenly asked,

"What the fuck are yo—?"

"Whaaaaaaaaaaaap!" It sounded as Haitian Fred stepped in and whacked the shit out of the cop.

"Knockout!" Haitian Fred shouted.

"Damn, son, you might have killed his ass!" Marc Dawg shouted.

"Okay, so you're gonna stand around and wait to see?"

Marc Dawg's eyes glared at him. "Hell nah, let's get the fuck out of here!"

They had just gotten to the door of the bando when Marc Dawg stopped dead in his tracks.

"Hold up!"

"For what?" Fred asked, looking left to right, right to left. He definitely didn't want to get caught inside an apartment with what looked like a dead cop.

"Got it!" Marc Dawg shouted as he came up to Fred at the door.

"Just follow me!" Fred said, turning to look him in the face.

Both men ran from the apartment, neither knowing if the cop was dead or not. All they cared about was getting as far away from the abandoned spot as possible.

When they arrived at the apartment where Big Zo and his men were staying, Marc Dawg began explaining the circumstances that led to him being chased by the police. In the meantime, Mo. Money was already on her way to pick his ass up from the projects.

***

Once Natasha had both phones in hand, she flipped one open and broke it, then tossed it into the ocean.

"Hey, that was my phone!" the young son shouted as he watched it float away.

"Don't worry, I'll replace that phone with a new one. Now please be silent while I make this call." She dialed a number. The phone rang twice while Dwight and his son pondered over who exactly they had on board their fishing boat.

"Hola!" a voice answered.

"This is Natasha. Where is my father?"

"Natasha! I'm so glad to hear your voice. Is everyone okay?"

"Thank you, it's nice to hear your voice as well. But not all is good. Now, where is my father?"

"Him and the family are having dinner with Mr. Valentino," the man said.

"Which Mr. Valentino?" she asked, looking at Dwight and his son. Their faces turned perplexed as they glanced between her, Miguel, and Maria.

"The one who signed over his soul to your father."

"I see. Well, tell him it's me."

"Yes, right away, señorita!" the man replied, then rushed into the large dining room.

On the other line, Natasha kept her eyes locked on the two men.

"So, are you all in some type of trouble?" Dwight Spears asked, hoping they wouldn't lose their lives for saving theirs.

"Not yet, but the coast guard cannot know anything about us. We were being chased by the Jacksonville Police Department when my sister decided to fly over the Bermuda Triangle. That's when our plane went down."

"Wait a minute, my young son found this," Dwight said, pulling out the piece of wreckage young Dwight had discovered.

"So is this part of your plane?" he asked.

"Yes. It belongs to the Pierre Santiago family."

"Oh shit!" Dwight shouted in disbelief.

Dwight Jr. didn't know what to think when he heard his father's words. He asked with excitement in his young voice, "Who is the Pierre Santiago family, Father?"

"Just one of the most feared drug cartels on the planet," Dwight Sr. replied.

"I beg to differ, sir. We are a close-knit family first. That's why it is very critical the coast guard not find out we were ever here. Do you understand, sir?" Natasha's eyes pierced him.

"Yes, I understand. Just don't hurt me and my son." He spoke as if begging for his life.

"What makes you think we—or I—want to harm you and your son?"

"I've heard rumors about the way your family operates."

"Please don't believe everything bad you've heard about the Santiago family. If someone died at our hands, they had it coming for crossing my father." Her eyes stayed locked on him and his son while Miguel and Maria sat silently.

"We won't," Dwight assured.

"Good. Once we are back home, safe and sound, your family will be compensated for your troubles."

"No charge, consider this a token of our good heart."

"Nonsense. No good deed goes without some type of monetary gain," she said, still waiting for her father to answer.

**

The family and my brother sat around the living room, enjoying casual conversation after dining on smothered pork chops, collard greens, mac and cheese, yellow rice, and fried chicken.

"Excuse me, Señor Santiago, you have a telephone call," one of the servants said as Pierre took the Cuban cigar out of his mouth.

He looked at his family and house guests and quickly uttered, "Please excuse me while I take this call."

While Pierre walked away, Firstborn couldn't focus on the conversation. He was too busy calculating numbers in his head, frantically trying to think of people he could sell the yayo to back in Tallahassee.

Ten minutes later, Pierre returned. His face no longer looked the same as when he left to take the call. Countess noticed the worry on her father's face. She stood to her feet.

"Father, you don't look good. What's wrong?"

He sighed, then looked at the few men gathered around.

"The crew of the plane have been found," he said softly.

"Hell, that's good news! Why the sad face, Mr. Santiago?" Firstborn unwittingly asked as he stood and walked over to him.

Pierre gave my brother a disgusting look, then said, "Everyone has been rescued, but Rhynyia."

"Oh God, no!" his wife shouted.

"What? What happened to her?" Countess asked.

"I only got small details from her sister," Pierre said, then continued. "My men are still out searching for her. But in the meantime, my men tell me that you guys were followed back to the airport…"

Chapter 33
Goodbye Camisha!

Speaking of the Hot Girls, while Camisha and I were talking, Nicole walked into the foyer, dressed in a Shakina Giovanni black dress, looking like a million dollars.

"Excuse me, Michael, it's getting late. We still have an hour and a half drive."

My head swiftly snapped around to see how beautiful she looked standing there.

"Thank you, my dear." I turned back to Camisha, who was standing there looking at her as well as I was.

"She must be the one that you're fucking?"

"Now why do you say that?"

"I can tell by the way she looks at you. Not to mention by the way she calls your name."

I must admit, she was right about a lot of things. Nicole must've heard her, because she stopped at the center of the stairs and said:

"No ma'am. I'm the one he's making love to. Now do I need to put an outfit together for you, Michael?"

My face held a side smirk as I stared at her beauty.

"Yes."

When I turned back to Camisha, I could see the look of dejection on her lovely face.

"I see that I can't compete with your new line of work, so I'm going to let you stay here with your hoes."

"They're not hoes, Camisha. They're dancers. And before you go, it was you who pushed me into this line of work."

"How so?" she asked, arms crossed over her chest.

136

"Remember all those times that you and your girlfriends left me at home to babysit their kids and yours while you all went to see the *Chip and Dales*?"

A warm smile broke out on her face as she replied:

"But like I told you, Michael, whenever I came back home from the show, I would want to make love to you."

"Yeah, you sure did. But you also told me that you would put my face on their body and think that they were me. What kind of shit is that to tell me!" I was in my feelings as I stood there staring at her.

"But Mi—" she tried to say.

"But my ass. Goodbye, Camisha."

***

It was late in the evening up in Jacksonville, FL. The police had been contacted a few hours earlier by one of the members of my group. They were told that Malik and I were running an escort service, and that a few of the girls were prostituting while Malik and I were receiving all of the proceeds. This was a blatant lie if I ever heard one. But that didn't matter to the Jacksonville Police Department. Once they got the info, they put together a task force just to arrest me and the girls—all because one of the females in the group couldn't have her way…

Meanwhile, Trigger was putting together a task force as well. He had already enlisted one lame nigga. Now he was over at one of his trap spots, talking with a few more brothers that didn't have anything else better to do but lose their life.

The spot was a bando at the end of Washington Street. Trigger was on the porch, surgically pulling on a rolled-up cigarillo. The kush he was smoking smelled good, tasted even better, as he blew out billows of smoke into the air.

"So you want us to kill a few bitches, because you think they whacked ole boy and a few of his friends?" Shorty Rock asked as he held his hand out for the kush-filled blunt.

"Basically. But what I want to do is get that one hoe, Lil Kitty, by herself, then make the bitch tell us who was behind the murder of my man."

"Lil Kitty?" Shorty Rock asked hesitantly, like he'd heard the name before.

"Yeah, Lil Kitty. You know her or something?" Trigger asked, staring at the short-in-stature man.

You see, Shorty Rock was given his street nickname because of his height. He stood four-foot-four, solid as a tree stump. In other words, a midget—though some prefer "dwarf." He probably weighed about a hundred and forty-five pounds, with a very large cranium.

The sole purpose of Trigger enlisting the man was his rep. Shorty was known to have an arsenal of weapons at his disposal. And that's exactly what Trigger needed. Once he had the right weapons, he would then gather up a few do-boys to carry out the mission.

"Yeah, come to think about it, I have. But where?" Shorty asked, gazing up into the sky.

"Probably over at the club," Trigger spat as he took the blunt back.

"Hell yeah, over at that hole-in-the-wall spot, Black Magic." Shorty said as he grabbed his crotch. "Yep, same place my boy must've met her and them tricks she be dancing with."

"Wow, my nigga, you ain't talking about the Florida Hot Girls, are you?" Short asked with a disgusted look on his face.

"Hell, I don't know who them hoes are she dances with. All I know is her number was in my boy's phone."

"Well I know for a fact she dances with that group. They be at that spot almost every other weekend. Your boy Malik even be having a radio commercial telling everybody they're gonna be in town."

"So you know how this trick looks?"

"Do I? Yeah, my nigga. She 'bout this tall." Short said, raising his short-ass arm. "And she got a nice lil tight ass. You know what?"

The short brother paused, trying to get himself together. The weed and the thought of Lil Kitty had him fucked up.

"Say it, my nigga. What's wrong with yo black ass?"

"She looks exactly like Chili from the group TLC. Even better if you ask me." Shorty Rock told him as he jumped down off the porch.

"Oh yeah? Well when I get her ass up here, I'm gone find out how well she can take all this pipe!" Trigger said, grabbing his dick.

"Whatever, my nigga. But what are you gonna do about them hoes she dances with? Rumor has it Punkin died because he and his friends got their hoes' timing off. Matter fact, every time somebody does something foul to them females, they end up over there at Claude's Funeral Home. You ready to die?"

Trigger looked at the midget as he pulled out a snub-nosed .38 special.

"Well you might be, but not my short black ass!" Shorty Rock said, just about to walk away from the bando.

"So what, you don't want to ride for the brother?"

What Short said next gave Trigger his answer.

"Man, fuck that dead-ass nigga!"

Trigger stood there on the porch, not believing the nonchalant attitude his lil homie was displaying.

"I should shoot that short-ass nigga in the back of his big-ass head," he mumbled as he watched the man walk out the yard.

"If it was you laying over at Claude's, you'd want your homies out spinning the block for you!" Trigger shouted.

"How could I? My lil short black ass would be dead! Just like you and whoever else is dumb enough to go after whoever did them niggas!" Short shouted back, then stopped and turned around.

"Just leave shit alone, Trigger."

"I can't! That nigga was my dude! And I'm pretty sure if it was me at Claude's, he would do the same for me."

"Well don't worry, you fuck with them females, it won't be long before your ass is over there. Matter fact, you might be buried right along with him and them other stupid-ass niggas!" Shorty Rock said.

"Fuck you, Shorty Rock!" Trigger shouted.

"Nah, my nigga. Fuck you! You're already the dead one!"

Those words hung in the stale air as Trigger pondered his decision to hunt down those responsible for Punkin's death.

If only he'd taken heed to what Shorty Rock was trying to tell him. Maybe then he could've prolonged his departure. But for one Martevious Leonard Hankerson, aka Trigger, he had a date already scheduled for himself at Claude's Funeral Home.

And the Murder Queens were going to make sure he made it.

Chapter 34
San Juan International

Firstborn didn't know what to ask first, so he just went for it. "So, do they think she's still alive?"

Pierre just stood there, blank stare on his face. "Right now, everything is sketchy. But if she's out there, my men will find her," he told him.

Then he looked at him and said, "What makes you so sure you guys weren't followed?"

"We didn't have a tail on us until we arrived at San Juan International."

"I'm not talking about when you all arrived in San Juan."

"Huh?" Firstborn asked, confusion on his face.

"You guys were followed ever since you left Florida," Pierre said.

"What? We followed the plan right down to the T!"

"Apparently not. But no problem. This is what we're going to do—you guys take a commercial flight back home. I'll have another one of my planes bring over the two hundred kilos tomorrow. Meet them at the airport so you can load up the cocaine. And this time, make sure you're not followed. No one will know the place or the drop-off time but you and me. Understand?" he asked, his stern look never breaking.

"Yes, sir," Firstborn replied, not even trying to figure out who had been tailing them.

"Give me a moment while I speak with my men," Pierre told him as he walked away. He needed to be alone for a few minutes. With the news about his family heavy on his mind, there was no way he could discuss business while Rhynyia was still missing.

There was no way she had perished at sea—not her. She had too much resilience in her. Out of all his children, Rhynyia was the one he needed by his side.

"There's no way my Rhynyia is not alive!" he said as he walked into his office.

While he was away, Firstborn walked up to his two amigos, winking at them. I guess he was trying to assure them that everything was alright.

"So, who is Rhynyia?" Fabian asked, his mind drifting from the large amount of kilos they were about to receive.

"She's the top dawg around here—not to mention the female my brother is engaged to."

"What? Mike is engaged?" Twan asked, mouth agape.

"Yep. Engaged to the female right there," Firstborn said, pointing at her picture on the wall.

"Damn, she's cute as a muthafucker," Fabian muttered.

"Yes, she is. I'm dating the other one, right there." He pointed at Natasha's picture.

"Okay, she's fly too. So are you gonna just stand here or call Mike and let him know about his girl?" Fabian asked.

"Damn, that's a good question," Firstborn said, mind on all the drugs he was about to have. Not one bit concerned about my girl… nor my feelings.

***

The ride to Gainesville was quiet, with only a few small conversations between the ladies. I wasn't concerned about their small talk—I had other things on my mind. I still hadn't heard from Rhynyia, didn't know if they had been rescued. My head was cloudy. Then there was Camisha stopping by, trying to convince me to come back home.

Yeah, right. Give up living in a house full of beautiful, butt-naked women? Who was I fooling? Who the hell did she think she was? At that moment, I was living any man's fantasy. And I wasn't thinking about walking away. But like most stories you read, all good things must come to an end. And mine was just around the corner.

Inside my truck that night, up in the front seat, I could hear Mo Money telling Nicole about what had happened with her brother, Marc Dawg. I would've wanted to hear too, but the female seated behind me was mean-mugging the back of my head. Her lil beady eyes were so menacing I had to ask.

"Lil Kitty, why you mean-mugging me?"

Her face didn't have the usual smile. Arms crossed against her small breasts, she took a deep breath and exhaled.

"For some odd reason, I can't get a hold of Punkin. Like I told you earlier, some of the girls say your girl Mignon was the last one to see him."

"Who told you that?" Mignon asked, glaring at her.

"Chyna told me."

Chyna sat in the back seat, looking like, *"Nah, bitch! I didn't tell you that so you could tell them I said it!"*

All eyes turned her way. She parted her thin lips and said, "What I was saying, Lil Kitty, is that I saw her talking to him. What happened to his short ass after that is a mystery to me."

With her mouth twisted, Lil Kitty shot back, "They know what I'm talking about." Referring to me and the girls, I guessed.

At this point, I knew things were about to get crunk. So I stepped in. "Listen, Lil Kitty, it's not that serious. If you can't get in touch with the man, just let it go. We'll see him when we go back up there."

I should've kept that to myself. Because what happened next was the beginning of the end.

"About Jacksonville, Mike—when we going back up there anyway?" Chyna shouted.

"I don't know right now, Chyna. With the way our schedule keeps changing, it's hard to pinpoint a date and time."

"No problem. When you do find out, please let me know," she muttered.

"Yeah, will do. Now, if you ladies will just go ahead and concentrate on tonight's show, I'm pretty sure we can put everything else behind us," I told them, pulling off the second Gainesville exit, eager to get to the club.

On the passenger side, Nicole casually turned to look back at Lil Kitty. "Don't worry, Kitty. I'm sure he'll call you sooner than later."

"If he don't, I'm pretty sure his boy Trigger will."

"Who?" Mignon asked, her face twisted up.

"Some dude named Trigger. His ass been trying to get me up there since yesterday," she said.

Mignon cut her eyes over at me. That's when I made a mental note to speak with Lil Kitty real soon. What I should've been doing was paying closer attention to the snake in the truck with us that night.

Chyna had just asked me when the next trip to Jacksonville would be. Right then, I should've questioned why she needed to know. But I didn't. I thought nothing of it. Years later, it all comes clear how she set me and the girls up. I was too far gone to see it.

***

When we pulled up to the nightclub, the line was already wrapped around the corner. The sight of the crowd instantly changed the mood inside my truck. I guess the huge turnout gave them a sense money was about to flow.

"Damn, this shit packed already!" JK shouted in that squeaky-ass voice of hers.

"Sho is. I'm 'bout to make me a nice chunk of bread tonight!" Lovely shouted, the thickest chick in the group.

144

"Me too, Lovely," her partner Suga Bear chimed in, glancing at her sister Chazz. "Yo, Chief Smoking Head—wake that ass up! We here!"

"I'm not sleep. I was just resting my eyelids!" Chazz said, wiping saliva from her lips, looking around like she'd been in a dream.

"Who they say gonna be here tonight again?" Peekachu asked, moving her small head around her thick neck.

"If you took time to look up at the sign, you'd see it says: *The Ying Yang Twins, featuring The Florida Hot Girls in the main room*," Nicole said.

All heads turned to confirm.

"Oh shit, it sure does! Mike, we done made it, playa—we some real-life celebrities now!" Mo Money shouted.

I looked over at her. "Yeah, that we are, young ladies. That we are. Now get your things together while I go see where we're gonna enter the club."

"Yes, sir. And make sure we got security to assist us inside. Some of them niggas out there look mighty thirsty," Strawberry chimed as I prepared to exit.

"Okay, Strawberry. I'll make sure I grab a few security guards," I said to the truckload of beautiful women.

Nicole would tell me later that as soon as I closed the door, Chyna told her, "I wouldn't worry about that, since them females called The Murder Queens somewhere around here."

Nicole whipped her head around. "Why you say that, Chyna?"

"Because Mike never leaves home without them."

"Oh, really?" Nicole asked.

"Yes, really. And if you ask me, those same females might know where Lil Kitty's friend is."

Chapter 35
A Strong Man!

I wish Chyna had never voiced her opinion that night inside my truck. Simple reason was, as soon as I came back with three huge security guards, Lil Kitty was outside demanding some type of answer about Punkin.

"Yo Rich, have your girls grab their bags and follow right behind that one security guard right there."

He staggered back over to the driver's side of his truck and made the announcement.

Meanwhile, Lil Kitty walked up to me. "So, are you ready to talk to me now?" She had her hands on her small hips, a smile on her face.

"Lil Kitty, there's really nothing to tell you. Why don't you give it a rest already? If the man wanted to speak with you, he would call you."

"You think so?" she asked as I tried to walk away.

"Listen, Kitty, think about it like this—why does he wait to see you whenever you're in town? If the man really liked you, he'd be on that ass all the time, not just when you get to Jacksonville."

She stood there looking up at me. "You think so?" she asked again, all sincere, like she was eating every word out my mouth. For some odd reason, I had that effect on a lot of women. My father always told me I inherited my charisma and charm from him—something that would propel me into the panties of plenty of women.

"Yes, Lil Kitty. You must not realize how attractive you are. And you really shouldn't play yourself anything shorter than that."

I spoke softly, my hand under her chin. She looked at me with sad, puppy-dog eyes. At that moment, I honestly believe I could've talked her right out of her moist panties. I knew this because of what she asked me next.

"Well, if I'm that cute ass female you profess me to be, why don't you have me as your leading lady?"

I cut her a shy, wicked smirk and was just about to answer when we both heard:

"Ummh, ummh! Excuse me, you two, but we do have a show to perform at. And besides, Mike, more than Lil Kitty needs your undivided attention right now."

I didn't have to turn around to know who it was blocking me from blowing Lil Kitty's back out right there.

"Okay, Mignon, I'm on the way!" I shouted, then whispered to Lil Kitty, "We'll finish this later."

"We better—'cause you got my pussy soaking wet," she replied, still smiling. She quickly grabbed her things and walked past me, swaying her lil hips side to side, making sure I noticed.

I fixed my shirt and started past Mignon, but she swiftly reached for my arm.

"Don't make me fuck her lil ass up!"

I looked at her, surprised. "What are you talking about, Mignon?"

"Alright, Michael. Play stupid if you want to. I know what was about to happen next," she said, staring dead in my face. She was so close I could smell the butterscotch candy on her breath.

"Nothing was about to happen, so stop tripping."

"Well, in that case, why is John Boy awake and standing at attention?"

Both our eyes went down to see what she was talking about.

"That's because he heard your pleasurable voice," I replied. "Now give me one of those butterscotch."

She pretended to dig in her pocket, then poked out the one already in her mouth. "Here—you can have the rest of this one."

You all know what happened next…

***

Firstborn didn't say a word for a moment, standing like his mind was elsewhere.

"Yo man, did you hear what I just asked you?" Fabian pressed, staring at a confused Firstborn.

"Yeah, I heard you. But if I call him and tell him, his ass might cancel the show I got planned for this weekend."

"What show, my nigga?" Fabian asked, surprised.

"The show I'm throwing this weekend."

"You throwing a concert or something?" Twan chimed in.

"Nah, fam. I told Mike to load up the trucks and bring as many of them strippers as he could. I'm 'bout to throw the wildest stripathon west Florida ever witnessed!"

"Word?" both brothers asked in unison.

"Hell yeah. For two days straight, I'ma have females up in Madison, Florida—throwing pussy and ass everywhere! And between the three of us, we gone be fucking and serving niggas from all over," he told them as they stood near the mantle where the sisters' pictures hung.

"Now I see why you don't wanna call him," Twan said, looking at my brother.

"You feel me?"

"We do. But don't you think he needs to know? She is his fiancée," Twan pressed.

Firstborn gave him a hard look. "Right now, I can't let nothing interfere with us making this bread. Or do you need to stay here, so Pierre can hang you up for them hogs to eat on your two-dollar ass?"

"Nah, son. Not at all. Let's get this money then," Twan said quickly.

"I thought so," Firstborn said as the room erupted when Natasha, Maria, and Miguel walked in.

***

Off in his private study, Pierre Santiago wasn't taking the news of Rhynyia's disappearance lightly. The man was a mess, sitting at his mahogany-stained desk. Head in hand, a glass of Cognac by his side, he felt pain he had never known.

Pierre Santiago was a strong man—physically, mentally. But at this moment, the world was crumbling down on him, fast. He had just lost his only son, Naheed, the one meant to take over the family business. Now, on top of that, came the news about Rhynyia.

She was supposed to be next in line if Naheed couldn't fill his shoes. And now, both of them were gone.

"Who am I going to look to, so they can run the family business?" he muttered, downing the Cognac before pouring another.

"I've worked so hard for my family to have generational wealth," he said aloud, as if someone was there with him. But the only company he had was the glass and expensive bottle of Cognac—until he slid open the drawer on his right side.

Inside the hidden compartment was a large amount of what he sold.

Tears flowed down his face as he leaned forward, head falling straight into the white powdered substance. At that moment, Pierre succumbed to the very thing he inflicted on so many innocent people…

Chapter 36
Life Is Too Short!

The white powder on the table looked too inviting. Trigger sat there, eyes bloodshot from smoking Kush, staring at it. Shorty Rock had left him alone after warning he'd be next—dead from fucking with the wrong females.

"Fuck that nigga and them hoes!" Trigger barked, lining up a thick rail of coke. He told himself a few bumps would clear his head.

Without hesitation, he rolled a dollar bill and snorted the whole line.

"Snnnnnnnn!" His wide nose sucked it up like a vacuum. You'd think after one hit he'd chill, but not Trigger. He went for another. And another. Before he knew it, two hundred dollars' worth of product was gone.

Problem was—it wasn't his. He mostly sold weed, sometimes coke on consignment from a local plug with bricks on hand. He'd only cop ounces here and there, telling himself he didn't have the clientele to move weight.

But now? He was in the back room of the bando, blowing through the man's stash. His heart thumped so hard it felt like it was about to tear through his chest. He was terrified of what was coming. Only way he saw himself winning was with an army behind him.

Same way Marquise rolled deep with hitters. But if Trigger could've gone back in time, maybe Marquise would've told his young ass that even an army of shooters couldn't save him from what was coming…

***

All the way to the club, Marsha's mind spun on Marc Dawg. From the short time she'd spent with him, she swore there was a connection. Not just the way he laid pipe, but something deeper. Still, jealousy gnawed at her—thinking about her stank-breath friend gobbling him up.

"I hope you got money for this cab, since your boyfriend left us broke," Candance snapped, her foul breath hitting the air. When Marsha zoned out again, Candance nudged her. "Yo, you hear me?"

Marsha blinked back from her daydream, then turned to her friend with her nose scrunched. "My bad. What you say?"

"I said, I hope you got money to pay the cab."

Without hesitation, Marsha slid out a twenty. "Yeah, I got this. How much is it?"

Candance's eyes widened at the roll of bills Marsha pulled. She was too busy staring to answer.

"Yo, chick, where you get all that money from?"

Marsha thought quick—no way she could tell her Marc Dawg left it. Trick's trifling ass would claim half since she "put in work." Which, to be fair, she did. Dude had smashed her in every position imaginable, then made love to Marsha like she was the only one in the room.

When he nutted, he even made Candance open her mouth to take it like a squirrel. She barely had time to gag before he was halfway down her throat.

Marsha snapped her friend back to reality. "Damn, Trick, you asking too many questions. I thought we needed money for this cab."

"We do, but where you get it from?"

Marsha sucked her teeth. "From dancing, Trick."

"You mean to tell me you made that much last night?"

"Yes. Why? How much you make?" Marsha asked, playing it off.

"Not that damn much," Candance muttered as the cab pulled up to Club Cleo's.

"Hopefully you make more tonight." Marsha handed the driver the twenty. "Keep the change." She slid out the back seat, but Candance stayed put.

"You can un-ass that change, playa. I need all that," she told the driver.

Stunned, he glanced back. "But she said—"

"Man, fuck all that. Gimme the change."

Once she pocketed it, she climbed out, stuffing the few bills in her bra. She looked around the lot. Only five cars sat there.

"Damn, ain't nobody here tonight," she said.

"I know, right." Marsha frowned as the cabbie cursed Candance out, screeched off, and nearly ran over Baby Lack pulling in.

Marsha stared her friend down. "No, you didn't."

"Yes I did. You out here with big money while I don't got a dollar."

"You got a few now, since you took my change."

"Whatever, hoe. He owed me that."

"Why?"

"'Cause while you had your head in La-La Land, I had these legs open and his ass was too busy staring at this pussy."

"Girl, you a trip."

"Whatever. I need money fast."

"Like I said in the cab, maybe you'll have a good night tonight."

"How, when it's only five cars in the lot?"

Marsha smirked, finger under her nose. "It's gonna get better. But what sandwich did you eat earlier?"

"Why?" Candance asked, covering her mouth.

"Because your lil mouth kicking."

Candance sniffed her own breath. "That's from that nasty dick I had shoved down my throat this morning."

Marsha almost cracked up.

"Yeah, he could've at least wiped it off. I just hope it wasn't no shit on it. I'd hate to get sick off your shit, bitch," Candance yelled just as Baby Lack walked up.

"What's good, ladies?" His lazy eyes locked on Marsha's praline ones. Something about her drove men wild.

"This sorry-ass club, that's what," Candance shot back, desperate for his attention.

"Yeah, kinda slow tonight, huh?" he said, still staring at Marsha.

"Real slow," Candance muttered.

"Maybe it'll pick up later." He tried to sound casual but wished Candance wasn't there cockblocking.

"It's already midnight and still dead. We need somewhere we know we'll make bread," Marsha cut in.

Baby Lack paused, then smiled. "You know what? I think I can help y'all with that."

He pulled out his phone and dialed a number…

Chapter 37
Baby Lack's Call!

It was about twelve-ten in the morning, and the club was jumping as the Ying-Yang Twins rocked the stage with *Salt Shaker*. The Florida Hot Girls were locked in the VIP, stacking bread. I was off to the side of the club, exchanging dollar bills, when my phone rang.

"Excuse me real quick, Nicole."

"Sure, bae," she said as I paused from counting her ones. It was early, and by the looks of her bag, she was bound to have a great night.

"Hello?"

"Yo Mike, this you?" the voice asked.

"Yeah, who else answering my phone?"

"My bad, Mike. It's me, Baby Lack."

I smiled at the sound of his name. Him calling meant one thing: the Florida Hot Girls' services were needed. I prayed that was the case. For some reason, I didn't want to take my ladies back to Jacksonville—not now, not anytime soon. I felt like something ugly was waiting for us, and I was too blind to see it. Like I said before, Lil Kitty would be in the middle of it, right along with the new chick, Candance. Why? Because both of them wanted fast money…

***

Meanwhile, back in Jacksonville, it was late. Only things open were chicken wing spots—and legs. Big Country had his face buried in his baby mama's thighs, tongue working her like a pro.

Her legs were spread eagle as he slurped and nibbled on her swollen clit. It was so big it looked like a midget's dick, half-hard. Didn't matter to Big Country—it turned him on.

The way he devoured her drove Courtney crazy. No man had ever pleased her like this. That's why she loved her mama's boy. What she didn't know? He was a beast with head, especially ass. The streets even crowned him #1 *Ass Eater*, a skill he picked up from his old boot camp partner, Roderick "Lil Hogan" Hogan.

Him and Lil Hogan spent nights in juvie talking about how to lock a woman down through her booty. At fifteen, Hogan was already a vet—three case managers at the facility were on his dick. He'd eat one out, she'd tell a friend, and soon he was running through the staff.

Hogan was short—five-seven, 150 pounds, light-skinned, high yellow. Folks swore he looked like Mike Tyson's twin. That theory got tested one day in the cafeteria.

Big Country had just arrived at the level-eight program, chopping it up with dudes from the bus. Lunch that day was chicken. Hogan stood in front of him and got the last piece.

"There you go, baby. Saved the last piece for you," Ms. Beasley, the cafeteria lady, said with a smile.

"Thank you, Ms. Beasley," Hogan replied smooth. She'd been sprung ever since he laid pipe and ate her ass better than any grown man could. She even called her man that night:

"You can pack your shit. This lil nigga done blew out my back!"

"What?!" Daniel King's heart dropped.

"No discussion. Lil Hogan ate my ass and stretched me with nine and a half inches of meat!"

Poor DJ was crushed.

Back in the line, Big Country saw Hogan get the last piece and reached for it. Wrong move. Hogan snapped off a vicious uppercut under his chin. Blood sprayed the wall.

"Oh shit!" Flash, a skinny dude nearby, yelled as Country stumbled. Hogan lit him up—three quick jabs to the gut, a smash to the jaw, then a two-piece to the temple that dropped the big kid cold.

Instead of chicken, Big Country ate the floor—and his own teeth.

His so-called boys? They scattered, never to be seen again.

After the hospital trip, Country, Flash, and Hogan became best friends. Hogan passed him the art of ass-eating, with one rule: always wash her booty yourself, so you know it's clean.

Country lived by that. Every time, he made sure. But not tonight. He'd been drinking heavy, mourning his father's death. The liquor had his sex drive on ten, and now his face was buried in Courtney's wet abyss.

"Umm, ahh, ohhh!" she cried out, squirting her third orgasm on his face. He licked up every drop like it was honeydew.

"You like that, don't ya?" he asked, head lifting from between her thighs.

She clutched his red afro, tears of pleasure streaming. "Do I? Please don't stop."

Courtney was gorgeous—six feet tall, 170 pounds, light skin, Chinese eyes, a knockout ass, and 34B cups. Perfect, except for the bum she had a baby with.

"I'ma make you nut one more time, then I'ma take this pussy," he mumbled.

"I don't care what you do—just eat this ass first," she moaned, face wet with tears.

In the next room, her sister Kendall was laid up. Kendall was a little shorter, just as fine, but she didn't care for nine-to-fives. She wanted her skrilla fast. The only way to feed her hunger was to show the world what she was blessed with. That's why she danced at Malik's club—Black Magic...

Chapter 38
Quenching Her Thirst!

Kendall had only been working over at Black Magic for a few nights, ever since she'd been kicked out of the Silver Fox strip club for slicing another stripper across her face. Silver Fox sat right down the road from Black Magic on Beaver Street. Word was, Kendall got put out because the female she cut had mistakenly scooped up a few of Kendall's dollars after dancing for one of her customers.

No charges were filed, and the police never got called. The club had already been dealing with a rash of problems inside, and the owner plus the manager weren't about to risk a violent crime getting reported. That kind of heat would shut the ritzy spot down for good. So instead, they banned Kendall. Which is how she found herself with a temporary home over at Black Magic.

"My goodness, you got the cutest pussy I've ever seen!" her customer told her, his grin stretched wide.

"I know, right? You can have some of this if your money long enough," she said, nibbling on the bottom of his earlobe.

"How much I need?" he shot back quick.

She gave him a gleaming look, though in truth she wanted to be anywhere else but that raggedy-ass club, shaking ass for cash. "I'd say about two to three hundred."

Without hesitation, he looked her dead in the eyes. "I got that all day, but I want to fuck your fine, pretty ass in your bed."

"Say less, my nigga." She gave a soft smile, standing up. "Let me get dressed, then we can head to my spot."

"No doubt," the young man said, watching her walk away, hips swaying side to side. "I'ma fuck the shit out her lil slim, red ass," he muttered, tugging at his dick. He couldn't wait to get between her legs.

***

I was seated off to the right of the VIP room, watching my ladies work the crowd. They were doing their thing heavy that night, and to me, things couldn't get no better. I'd just gotten off the phone with Baby Lack, who told me he had two new females wanting to dance with the Hot Girls. Music to my ears—new blood always meant fresh money.

But looking back now, years later, why didn't I see the writing on the wall then? I know you're asking yourself— see what? My answer: *loose lips sink ships.* The more females I let onto the team, the more hatred, jealousy, and disloyalty they dragged in. What I valued most ended up being the very thing that tore the Florida Hot Girls down and sent me away for a long time.

Don't get it twisted—some might think it was the Orlando females who brought us down. Nah. At least not to my knowledge. Yeah, a lot of women from Orlando danced with the Hot Girls—and still do to this day—but it wasn't them.

The ones who did this know exactly who they are. They still stuck in the same miserable-ass place they was in when I first met them. If I named them, they'd probably claim I made them legends, gave them street credit. But nah, not me. To them I say: **fuck you.** You were cold pieces of shit then, and in my eyes you still are. Once a rat, always a rat.

Out the corner of my eye, I spotted Lil Kitty chopping it up with two big dudes. At first glance, they looked like ordinary cats—but I knew better. She'd fucked up plenty shows and money in the past, but these two? They were about to erase all that… until the weekend we returned to Jacksonville.

She stood with them a long while before Nicole walked up to me.

"Hey you, want some company?"

"So what, you through dancing for the night?" I asked, turning my gaze away from Kitty.

"Who knows. But judging by my bag, I might as well be."

"Let me see." She held up her Crown Royal bag.

"Damn, Nicole, your bag full! How much you got in there?"

She smiled. "Not quite sure, but it's enough."

Mo. Money and Mignon walked up just then.

"So y'all done for the night too, I presume?" I asked.

"Kind of, sorta," Mo. Money said, looking like something was heavy on her mind.

"What that mean?" I asked, glancing from her to Mignon. Truth be told, I still wasn't over Mignon, and looking at her fucked with my head. She must've known, too, 'cause the lil heifer made sure I could see her fat-ass moose knuckle bulging through her outfit. Sticking out so far even Nicole caught it.

Nicole glanced down, then up at me, then back at Mignon before snatching her by the arm. "Chick, you don't see how the lips of your pussy 'bout to bust out your outfit?"

"What?" Mignon looked down, then back up with a surprised face. "Oh snap, I ain't even know," she told her, while I stayed locked on Mo. Money.

"So why the long face, girl?" I asked.

She kept quiet at first, just dropped her head.

"Please don't tell me you pregnant, Mo. Money."

"No Mike, it's something more serious than that," she finally said, lifting her head.

"Whew! What can be more serious than that? Shit, if you ain't pregnant, that's great news to me."

"No Mike, it's real serious," she repeated, staring at me. Whatever she had to say, it was heavy—her whole demeanor was off.

"Mo. Money, I can't read minds. Tell me what's eating at you."

"Remember when y'all picked me up and I smelled like—" she started, but Lil Kitty jumped in between us.

"Excuse me you two, but Mike, those two guys over there wanna speak with you."

Me and Mo. Money both looked down at her.

"Not now, Lil Kitty. Don't you see me talking?" I said.

Kitty turned to Mo. Money. She must've read her expression, 'cause Mo. Money cut her off quick. "Not now, Lil Kitty. Not now."

"But Mike, this real important—it's a lotta money at stake," she pleaded, eyes begging me to hear her out.

I sighed, glanced at Mo. Money. "Let me see what this about. Stay here, I'll be right back."

"Go ahead, Mike. I'll be here," she said.

I looked down at Lil Kitty. "If this about you leaving the club with these two big-ass niggas, the answer's no! I don't care how much money they got, neither one of 'em fucking my Lil Kitty."

"Whatever, Mike!" She laughed.

"I'm dead ass, shorty."

Chapter 39
Wow Lil Mama!

The whole time Lil Kitty and I walked over to the guys, she never dropped her gorgeous smile.

"Why you still smiling?" I asked.

"Because, Mike—when you see what these guys want, you gonna love me."

"Am I gonna make love to you, or you to me?" I smirked, sneaking a peek at her lil goldmine behind her. Like I always said—Kitty was slim and petite—but she knew how to work that lil booty. And she must've worked it so good, these two dudes needed to speak with me about it.

Turns out, the two cats in the club that night with the Ying-Yang Twins were up-and-coming rappers themselves.

"You must be Mike, the manager and owner of the world-famous Florida Hot Girls?" the first big fella asked, holding out his hand.

"That depends on who's asking," I shot back, taking his hand.

"Well, in that case, nice to meet you. My name's Derrick, and this here's my partner Maurice."

"Nice to meet you, Maurice. Derrick." I nodded, pulling my hand back.

I looked down at Lil Kitty. Her smile was wider than ever, proud of herself for bringing me over. I didn't know what to expect, but what I was about to hear was exactly what I needed. What these guys were about to propose would give me and the Florida Hot Girls a major push over all obstacles.

We were about to become superstars and didn't even know it.

But just as I was about to get good news from them, bad news was brewing elsewhere—and I had no idea what was coming.

***

Miles away, down at the bottom of the map, a beautiful young stripper was leaving Club Cocoa's. At the time, Cocoa's was one of the hottest spots around. I'd taken my girls there when I first started in the business—a big mistake.

That first night, a few of my ladies were flat-out terrified, not sure if they could even perform there. On top of that, some of them didn't even have the $100 bar fee required before they could dance. Guess who had to pay it? Me. My black ass. So yeah, I was pissed.

The manager explained it was because I brought them on a weekend, meaning they had to pay the higher fee since they were taking spots from regular girls. I was disgusted, ready to haul their scared asses back to Orlando and let them dance in hole-in-the-wall joints. But Ms. Kitty, as usual, talked me into staying. At the time, I was still eating out her hands, so I agreed.

It was my first time stepping into the big leagues, and I was about to see how it was really done. I sat in the corner, waiting on my ladies, and realized quick—this wasn't Tampa. Hell nah. Cocoa's was different.

Females strolled the floor naked. The stage dancers started clothed but stripped down by the third song. The floor itself was covered in money—you couldn't even see the tile.

When my girls finally came out, Kitty led, looking flawless. The rest trailed behind like they'd stepped into the wrong damn world. Monique especially—by the time I reached her, she was shaking.

"What the hell's wrong with you?" I asked, looking every bit the Kansas City pimp.

"I'm scared, Mike. Look at all these people," she whispered, trembling.

I glanced around and knew right then—I was out of my league. Standing next to Monique was a bad-ass female, damn near naked. I checked her top to bottom, about to ask if she wanted to go somewhere private. But right in front of her stood a short, stocky dude with stacks of ones in his hand.

I wondered how he was gonna pay her. Didn't take long to find out.

"I'm 'bout to make it rain on your fine ass, mama!" he shouted, tossing a hundred ones in the air before walking off without a care.

I was so caught off guard I almost started picking them up. Thought better of it, turned to Monique. "Better get you some of that money," I told her, eyes wide as Buckwheat from *The Little Rascals*.

She shook her head. "That's her money, Mike."

"Damn, my bad. Well, you better get like her, or you gonna be left here broke." I stormed off, mad as hell I'd even brought them. Head down, I didn't notice what was happening outside at first.

When I finally looked up, four dudes were stealing our rental van.

"Goddamn!" I shouted, sprinting toward them. "Hey, that's my shit!"

"It's our shit now, nigga," one barked, waving a handgun. "You can die right here or walk back inside."

I spun on my heels, fast. First person I saw near the front of the club was a tall Dade County cop directing traffic. Problem was, I had no license and three warrants. I damn sure didn't want to go to jail down here. Still, I ran up on him.

"Excuse me, officer, those guys stealing our van."

The brother stood six-four, looked down at me, and said, "And what the fuck you want me to do?"

I was so dejected all I could mutter was, "Never mind, officer. Thank you."

That awful weekend ended with us catching flights home. All the money I made got spent on plane tickets.

***

That memory must've been weighing on one female's mind as she walked out of Cocoa's. Her heart wasn't in it anymore. She still wanted to dance and make money, but she was homesick. She wanted to be back among the girls she knew. All she needed was to make that call.

She slid into her roommate's car, face heavy. Her friend caught it instantly.

"What's wrong? Why the long face? You ain't make no money tonight?"

She lifted her head slow from her friend's chest, eyes misty. "I'm kinda homesick. I think I wanna go back home."

"Oh really? Or do you just miss being with him?"

Her face turned away. "Please don't mention his name. He too busy with his precious Rhynyia to even think about me."

"Damn, you must not watch TV," her friend said.

"Why you say that?" she asked, wiping the last of her tears.

"I don't know how to tell you this, but… that girl and her family went down in a terrible plane crash a few days ago."

"Oh no! He must be devastated!" she screamed.

"I don't know. Maybe you should give him a call, Ms.—"

Chapter 40
Home!

The two light knocks startled Pierre at first, causing him to look up with a dazed, confused glare.

"Yes, who's there?" he shouted, wiping his face clean of the cocaine residue. No one knew about him partaking in his own supply—and no one needed to know. This was his business. Besides, he needed to clear his head.

"It's me, Father. Can I come in?" the pleasant sound of her voice asked.

"Yes, you may enter," he yelled, as Natasha walked into his study.

"I'm sorry, Father, but we tried to find her—"

She tried to say more, but he cut her off by placing his index finger up to his lips.

"No worries, my dear. Your sister will be found, I can assure you that."

"How can you be so sure, Father?" Natasha asked.

"Trust me. If I know her like I do, I know that she's still alive."

Natasha lowered her head.

"I wouldn't be surprised if she wasn't out there right now, trying to get back home to us. Now—what can you tell me about what happened?" Pierre pressed.

But just when Natasha went to speak, the door of her father's study swung open.

"Father, we only have a small window for their departure. If they are to leave this morning, we have to get them there now!" Countess said, looking from Natasha to Pierre.

"I see. Make flight arrangements for them to fly back within the hour. Pay for their flight with this." He pulled a credit card from his jacket.

"Have Fernando take them back to San Juan International once they find out who it is following them."

"Then what?" she asked, standing firm in front of her father.

"Once they've been found out—dispose of them the only way you know how." An evil grin slid across his face.

"Yes, Father." Countess turned, then looked over at Natasha. "I'm glad that you're back home with us." Her face was as stern as their father's.

"Me too. But I won't be complete until Rhynyia returns as well," Natasha said, looking between her father and Countess.

"Countess, go ahead and make the flight arrangements while I speak with your sister."

"Yes, Father."

As Countess turned on her heel, Pierre leaned in, staring into Natasha's lovely face.

"Now please—tell me what happened."

Just as he asked, Natasha began to explain everything, and why they had to fly over the Bermuda Triangle...

***

The club was so loud and amped up, I had to ask the two big guys if we could talk somewhere more private. They agreed, so I told Lil Kitty to give us a few minutes. I didn't need her in my business.

Once we stepped outside, I was the first to speak.

"Okay fellas, what's on your mind?"

"Your Florida Hot Girls are what's on our minds," Maurice said.

"How so, big fella?" I asked with a side smirk, not quite ready for what he was about to drop.

"Well, Mr. Mike, we're part of the rap group that sings *'Wow Lil Mama.'* And we want you and the Florida Hot Girls with us down in Miami next week."

I stood there with my mouth wide open.

"What was that again?" I had to ask twice.

"Next weekend is the rappers convention down in Miami. We're performing with a host of other rappers and groups. We need your girls there with us—on stage while we're performing."

"Man, do you know how many females I got in this group?"

"We don't care how many," Maurice said. "Just make sure every one of the females here tonight comes with you next weekend."

"That's a lot of females. What about the—"

Derrick cut me off, pulling out a stack of big bills.

"Here's enough money for their hotel rooms." He slapped two thousand into my hand. "And here's enough for you to bring them all to Miami." He rolled out another three grand.

My eyes locked on the money, then on both men.

"So y'all ain't playing, huh?"

"Hell nah! Like I said—we need them Florida Hot Girls on the scene, making sure they represent."

"No doubt. We'll be there," I said, shaking both their hands. "Hell, I wish the convention was this week."

"We do too, Mike," they said in unison as we walked back inside.

I was so happy and elated that this rap group wanted my girls, I couldn't wait to tell them the good news. But just as I stepped back in, Mo. Money stopped me.

"Mike, I desperately need to speak with you!" Her eyes were bloodshot red.

She gripped my arm so tight I thought she'd snap it.

"Damn, Mo. Money—is it that serious?"

"Yes, Mike." She looked up at me with a worried face.

"Okay, talk."

"Mike, I think we might be in trouble."

"Who the hell is *we*? Last I checked, *we* didn't kill anybody."

"For real, Mike?" she shot back, sarcastic.

"Yes, for real. Now what's the problem?"

She took a deep breath, then told me about her half-brother, Marc Dawg—and how the two dead bodies she'd acquired were supposed to be destroyed along with the dude's car. But for some strange reason, Marc Dawg didn't handle business. Instead, he wound up in a high-speed chase, ending at some apartments over on Mercy Drive.

"So that's what all that commotion was I heard earlier?"

"Yes, Mike. And when I went to get his dumb ass, the police had the entire complex locked down like Fort Knox."

"How so?"

"You couldn't get in or out," she said, eyes watering up.

"So what are you gonna do?" I asked, wanting no part of it.

She jumped back, staring at me with cold eyes.

"What do you mean, what am *I* gonna do? We're all in this shit together, Mike."

"Wait a minute. *We* didn't kill anybody, and *we* damn sure didn't get involved in no gotdamn high-speed chase with them crackers! So the way I see it, this is *your* mess. You gotta handle it."

"But how? And if one of us has a problem, don't we all have a problem?" she asked, pleading.

I let out a deep sigh.

"We do. But Mo. Money, what your half-brother did— that's on you and him. And what you think his black ass gonna do if and when he gets caught?"

She lowered her head, afraid to answer.

"Hello, I know you hear me?"

She looked up, dull-eyed. "Gee, Mike, I don't know." She shrugged, staring at me with puppy dog eyes.

"Well we do," Mignon cut in as she and Nicole walked up behind us.

"This nigga's gonna talk. And he's gonna tell them everything he can to save his own skin," Mignon said.

"Hey, where'd y'all come from?" Mo. Money asked, turning to them.

"From inside the club," Nicole said. "Now Mike, you go on back inside while we put something together out here. Besides, one of the Ying-Yang Twins is looking for you. Says they got a show down in Orlando in a few days."

I threw up a finger to stop her. "Let me guess—they want the Florida Hot Girls at that show too, huh?"

"Yes, baby," Nicole answered.

"That's if we're not in somebody's jail by then," I snapped, storming past Mo. Money.

If it wasn't one thing, it was always another lurking right around the corner for me and them damn Florida Hot Girls...

Chapter 41
Trapped Like a Caged Animal!

After the shooting, all officers had been accounted for—except one. The police department placed the Carver Shore Apartments on mandatory lockdown. The place was locked down tighter than Fort Knox. Officers went door to door, checking IDs and making sure people inside their apartments actually lived there.

No one could leave unless they were headed to work or had a hospital emergency. No one could enter unless they lived there. Whoever had been driving that car wasn't escaping. The department figured the driver had done something serious—that's why the chase had gone down in the first place.

That all made perfect sense to the lead officer as he watched the charred car being lifted onto a tow truck.

"Why did the person driving this car run from the law?" Officer Joseph Flanagan muttered, watching the driver work.

"That's a good question. Dispatch says the driver had outstanding warrants up in North Carolina," Officer Wilson said, walking up behind him.

Flanagan snapped his head around. "Hey Wilson, what the hell you doing out here?"

Wilson gave him a sharp look. "If the driver went so far as to run into the projects—and then blow the car up—he was covering something up." Both men turned to the burnt-out wreck.

"What is it, Wilson?" Flanagan barked.

"Did you guys really check the car?"

"They checked it as best they could. Look at that heap—there's nothing left!" Flanagan shouted.

"I think you better look again. Because if I'm seeing right... that looks like a bone. Somebody's arm—hanging off the back of the vehicle."

Flanagan stepped closer. His eyes widened. Then he lost it.

"Goddammit! It is an arm! Get the coroner over here now!"

***

Apartment 1256 was supposed to be abandoned. No one had lived there in a long time. At first, the lone officer and the apartment manager were going to skip it—until the manager noticed something off.

"So you claim all these apartments are unoccupied, correct?" the officer asked the frail-looking white man.

"That is correct... but there's a problem." The man looked at the officer, then back at the door. He pressed his bony finger against his lips. "Shhh. The door's slightly ajar. That can't be good."

The officer stiffened. "So that door should be locked?"

"Yes. No way it should be open," the man whispered, pushing his rimmed glasses higher on his face. His expression was pure fright.

The officer raised an arm, shielding him. "Stay behind me, sir. Our suspect might be inside."

The manager wasted no time sliding behind him, shaking like a leaf.

"Wait—aren't you going to call for backup?" he asked.

"No need. I got this," the officer said firmly, service weapon drawn.

"This is Officer Paul Halaburton with the Orlando Police Department! Come out with your hands up!"

Five seconds passed. Nothing.

"Stay here—I'm going in," Paul said. He shoved the door open and froze at what he saw. His hand shot to his radio.

"Officer down! I repeat, officer down! I'm at apartment 1256 with an officer down! I need medical and backup!"

They had just found the one missing officer. He lay sprawled on the floor—no gunshot wounds, no blunt trauma—but something was terribly wrong.

"Is he alive?" the manager whispered, hovering in the doorway.

"He's got a pulse. He's breathing—barely," Paul said, kneeling beside him, gripping his hand. His chest tightened. This wasn't just a fellow cop. This was his partner—his lover. They were supposed to be married in the spring.

"Hang in there, buddy. Don't you die on me," Paul whispered into his ear.

The manager stood frozen, sensing the two were close—but not *that* close. He found out quickly.

"You two must be good friends," he said nervously.

"Yes. Real close," Paul answered, still holding his partner's hand. "We're supposed to be married in the spring."

"Oh snap!" the frail man gasped. He stumbled back, bolted out of the apartment, and puked in the hallway. He was Arabian, and his culture forbade homosexuality.

***

Only four doors down sat Big Zo, Marc Dawg, and the rest of the crew involved in the Carver Shore mess. They were holed up inside a three-bedroom unit—the home of Big Zo's side piece, Cecilia Streets. She had three young sons who all thought Big Zo was their father. He wasn't, but he made sure to take care of them—and their mother.

Now, with police swarming just doors away, Cecilia and her boys were about to be ripped apart.

"Yo man, what the fuck we gonna do?" Haitian Fred panted, sweat dripping down his face.

"Be calm, my bruds. Lemme sort this thing out," Big Zo said, then glanced at Marc Dawg. He was pressed against the door, listening to the chaos outside.

On the couch, Cecilia sat crying. "I don't know why your big stupid black ass even agreed to help this nigga! Now look at us—trapped like runaway slaves!" she shouted.

"Listen, ma, I ain't mean for it to get like this. But I promise—when it's over—I'll take care of you and them boys." Marc Dawg clutched his Glock tight. He wasn't going out without a fight. Not tonight. If it came to it, he was ready to take a few cops with him.

Meanwhile, Big Zo was shut up in the back bedroom—praying. He'd been taught since a boy: whenever trouble showed its face, pray, and God would answer.

"Listen, Zo! I don't know what you're doing back there, but the boys in blue gonna be at this door in two minutes!" Chill Will yelled. No answer. He rushed down the hall, flung the last door open—

"Zo, I know you hear me!—oh shit! Where the fuck did that come from?"

Chapter 42
Her Story!

As Natasha told her side of the story about their flight, Countess did as instructed and went to make travel arrangements. Firstborn and his two goons needed to get off that island—fast.

They were waiting outside Pierre's office when Countess ran out, credit card in hand.

"So what's good?" one of them asked, grabbing her arm.

"We gotta get you back—that's what's good." She yanked away. "Now let go before my sister comes out here and sees you too close. You wouldn't want her to dispose of you that quick."

He dropped her arm fast. "It wasn't like that. I meant no harm."

"Me neither. But with what she's been through, you don't know her mental state right now."

"You're right."

"I know I am. Now let me do this and put together a plan for whoever's following you. My father gave me strict instructions—he wants them disposed of."

Her words hung in the air, then she was gone.

"I just hope it ain't like how they disposed of that poor family—fed to them hogs."

"You mean pigs," Fabian muttered.

"I don't give a damn if it was pigs or hogs—I just know I don't wanna be the next one ate."

"You got that right," Firstborn mumbled, standing close behind them, eavesdropping.

***

Inside Pierre's study, Natasha gave her father every last detail. He listened closely—until she said:

"So when she found out there was more of your product on board, she made adjustments."

Pierre stiffened. "What do you mean, *more* product, Natasha? Didn't Mr. Valentino take the thirty kilos?"

"Yes. He did. We all helped him pack it."

"Then where did more product come from?"

"That's what I was gonna ask *you*, father."

"I have no knowledge of this," he said, hands clasped behind his back. But even as he spoke, a voice replayed in his mind like a recording:

We're closer to you than you think, Pierre. The people responsible for your son's death—and yours as well—are closer than you think. We got people all around you. We can touch you whenever we see fit. Fuck you, puta!

He flinched at the memory of the man's words.

"Father? Father, do you hear me?" Natasha shouted, snapping him out of his trance.

"Someone inside my organization is working with the same people who killed my son," Pierre said, spittle flying.

"But who, father?"

"There can only be one. And that one has been right here all along." He stared into the soft eyes of his daughter…

***

Kendall and her trick had been back at her place about twenty minutes, sitting in the living room smoking. He had rolled up earlier. The blunt's aroma was loud—too loud—and not the usual weed smell. It stank. Kendall wrinkled her nose but kept smoking.

She pulled the blunt from her lips, squinted at him. "What you say this shit was again?"

He grinned. "Some new shit my cracker dealer John sold me." He passed it back. "Why, what's wrong?"

She shrugged, already high. "Nothing, just... smells different than any weed I ever smoked." She pulled hard, coughed until her chest rattled.

Her trick's eyes bulged. "You okay, gorgeous? Don't get sick on me before I give you this money." He pulled a fat wad of hundreds from his pocket and tossed it on the table.

Kendall's eyes lit up. *I'm 'bout to put it on his ass this morning, since he flashing all that cash,* she thought, reaching for it.

"Whoa, lil mama. You can have all that once you take care of this." He unbuckled his Wrangler jeans, pulling out what looked like a damn candy apple—with two gigantic balls hanging beneath.

"What the hell?" Kendall gasped.

"You know what it is, lil mama," he muttered, dragging her closer.

She blinked at his deformed length. "I'mmm... good... but this is—" She tried to finish, but the crack-laced blunt had her twisted. Her head bobbed, eyes glassy, too high to resist.

"Don't worry, big daddy got you," he growled, gripping the back of her neck and shoving her mouth down on him.

"Waaaiiitttt, I told you—" Her words cut off as he forced himself deeper. She had meant to say she didn't give head, but the way she was gagging and slurping on his swollen tip, no one would've believed her.

"Uhhh, ahhh, ummmh!" The wet sounds from her mouth pushed him closer to the edge.

"Damn, bitch, slow down before I bust all over your pretty face!" he snarled.

But she didn't slow. She pulled him out, gasping, "Oh shit, this dick so big!" Her thin hands barely wrapped around his girth as he slapped it across her face.

"If you think my shit big now, wait till I get inside that tight pussy! I'ma tear that shit up!" he grunted, staring at her.

"Well, what we waiting for? Come on—let's take it to my bedroom," she said, wobbling to her feet.

What she didn't know was the man's deepest, darkest desires. If she had, things might've turned out different for poor Kendall.

Chapter 43
Evil Intentions!

Just as Kendall stood to her feet, the man jerked the shit out of her arm. "Fuck that! I want this pussy right here, right now!"

The violent manner in which he grabbed her sent chills up her spine. Where was the kind man she had met earlier—the man she thought wanted to make love to her?

"But I thought you wanted me in my bed?" she uttered in protest, not knowing she'd soon be fighting for her life.

"I do, but I'm gon' bust my first nut right here!" he told her as he stood up fleetly, his Wrangler jeans and boxers dropping to the floor in one motion. The man was a pro at taking what he wanted.

"But wait, my sister might come out here and catch us!" she said as she sat there, rubbing her shoulder.

"Fuck all of that!" he yelped, pulling her up and ripping her thongs clean off her body. Kendall was curvaceous in every way a man could imagine.

With fire in his eyes, he tossed the ripped garments to the floor and turned her around, placing her body over the black leather sectional. Before she knew it, the man had all ten inches of his raw manhood engulfed inside her small vaginal walls.

She wanted to scream—the pain he was inflicting was unbearable—but she didn't want to wake her sister. "Uhhh, ahhh, ummmh! Please take it out, you're killing me! Plus you don't have on any protection!" she cried, turning her head back to look at him as he punished her. Sweat dripped down her face in heavy beads.

"Shut the fuck up! Didn't you tell me you wanted all of this dick?"

"Ummph, huh, yeah daddy. But not like this..." She didn't finish her sentence—he shoved her head down into the couch. Once she was pinned, he began an onslaught on her small womb. In and out, over and over, making sure she felt every inch of him.

For ten straight minutes he fucked the poor girl, who now had tears of pain in her eyes. Just when she thought it was over, he pulled out, then slapped on a Magnum condom.

"Oh, now your black ass wants to put on a condom?" she spat as he finally released her. "You know what, I think I've changed my mind. You can take your money and get the fuck out of my house!" She tried to search for her clothes, but his next words froze her in place.

"Bitch, you got T-Roy fucked up! Keep that little piece of change—'cause what I'm about to do to your small ass rectum, you gon' need it to help pay for your hospital bill!"

Oh shit, she thought, trying to jump up from the couch.

"Whaaaap!" Too late. T-Roy was quick, slapping fire out her mouth. Her bottom lip swelled instantly. When she realized she was bleeding, she tried to scream.

"Baaaaaaaap—baap—whaap!"

Before she knew it, everything went dark as her eyes slowly closed. With her body limp, T-Roy flung her over his shoulder and searched out her room.

Once inside, he laid her across the bed, still unconscious from the beating. "Yes-yes-yes! Now I'm 'bout to punish your lil thin ass booty. That'll teach you about teasing men with this small ass."

He bent her over, licked her asshole after sniffing it, then shoved ten inches where no man had ever been before.

"Ahhhhhhh, shit! This the tightest piece of ass I ever took!" he grunted, forcing himself into her locus hole.

Poor Kendall didn't know she had invited the serial killer who'd been murdering strippers after they left clubs across the city…

***

The club didn't close that morning until around 3 a.m. The girls had made a nice chunk of change and I couldn't wait to tell them the good news. Everyone had smiles on their faces as they dressed. I even wore a giant smile myself, since I had some good news too.

Right before I could speak, my phone rang again. I didn't recognize the number, but it had a 305 area code.

"Umph, I wonder who could be calling me from Miami?" I thought to myself, then turned back to the ladies.

"What's good, bae? Everything okay?" Nicole asked, walking up.

"Nothing, just need to speak with you ladies real quick." I nodded, then asked, "So how did things work out with Mo' Money?"

"It's all good. Me and my girl will explain later."

"Okay, that's what's up." She stood there staring at me.

"Now what's up with the news you have to tell us?"

"You know what, why don't I tell you when all the ladies are here?"

"Sounds good to me," she replied, then turned to the crew. "Excuse me ladies, Mike has something to tell you all!"

"Go ahead, bae."

"Thank you, Nicole. Like she said, I've got something to tell y'all. Thanks to your girl Lil Kitty, you're invited to Miami next week for the rappers' convention. Hotel rooms and expenses are covered."

"What? Nah, not the rappers' convention?" Suga Bear shouted.

"Yes ma'am. That's right. But before Miami, you got a bachelor party in Deland Friday night. Then we head out."

"What about this weekend?" Chazz asked.

"This weekend, y'all are booked in Madison, Florida."

"And when we going back to Jacksonville?" Chyna's voice carried through the room.

"I don't know, but with all these other shows, Jacksonville is the last place I want to take y'all."

"I wonder why?"

"What was that, Chyna?" The room grew quiet. She feared no one, especially me.

"I said, I wonder why."

"Because I said so, that's why. Now if you want Jacksonville so bad, go on your own. Back to you ladies—last but not least, the Ying-Yang Twins told me to tell y'all thanks for showing up and showing out tonight."

"They're welcome!" some of the girls shouted in unison.

"That's not it—they want y'all at their Orlando show in a few weeks. Now go on and get dressed, we got a long trip home."

"Why don't we grab some breakfast, then stay the night up here?" Peekachu asked.

"No sir, I gotta get back to my little princess."

"Hell, we thought she was here with you already?" Suga Bear laughed.

"Not this one, he talking about his daughter, Mykel," Nicole said.

"Thank you, Nicole. Now please, get dressed while I take this call." My phone still wouldn't stop ringing. Same Miami number.

I hesitated but answered. "Hello."

"Bout damn time you answered."

Soon as I heard her voice, I knew who it was. I just didn't know why she was calling. I hadn't heard from her since that weekend she got left in Miami.

"What's up?"

"You know what's up."

"No, I don't. Say what's on your mind, I'm trying to head home."

"Let me get straight to the point, I need to—"

Beep. Another call.

"Hold on."

"But Mike—"

Too late. I clicked over, thinking it was good news from my brother.

"Hello. Did they find them?"

"Yeah, baby boy. They found them, but…"

"How's Rhynyia? How's my baby?"

"Baby boy, I don't know how to tell you this." He choked up.

"Tell me what? Where you at? You with the family?"

"Yeah, I'm here now." I could hear Natasha in the background: *Let me tell him.*

"Hello! Hello!" I shouted. My voice was so loud Mignon, Nicole, and Strawberry came up beside me, like they already knew.

"Michael, it's me, Natasha."

A warm smile hit my face hearing her voice.

"Hey Natasha, where's my girl Rhynyia?" I asked frantically, desperate to hear her. The silence told me something was wrong.

"Michael… I don't know how to tell you this. But Rhynyia didn't make it."

Those were the last words I heard before everything went completely dark…

To Be Continued…

Location: Somewhere in the Atlantic Ocean.
Time: 6:25 a.m., Thursday morning.

Just before dawn, the large vessel *Siesta Key* was on the last leg of its journey. The men were tired after three weeks at sea.

The young man at the helm had been driving eight hours straight, fighting off sleep, when he noticed something floating off the starboard side. At first, he thought it was debris. But looking closer through binoculars, he knew his eyes weren't deceiving him.

"Captain! Captain! Alla, alla—una pequeña balsa, montón también nuestro exacto partido!"

The captain rushed up. "¿Cuántos pueblos percibes?"

"Imparcial uno—y ella busca en bonita mala forma!" the excited young man shouted as he steered toward the drifting raft.

No one knew if the person aboard was alive, but they knew one thing: they had to rescue them...

Lock Down Publications and Ca$h Presents
Assisted Publishing Packages

Due to an increase in the price of services we have increased our prices. The prices below reflect the price increase as of 11/1/24.

BASIC PACKAGE $699	UPGRADED PACKAGE $1000
Editing Cover Design Formatting	Typing Editing Cover Design Formatting Upload eBooks to Amazon Upload Paperback to Amazon
ADVANCE PACKAGE $1,400	**LDP SUPREME PACKAGE** $1,700
Typing Editing (line editing/content) Cover Design Formatting Copyright Registration Proofreading Upload eBooks to Amazon Upload Paperback to Amazon	Typing Editing (line editing/content) Cover Design Formatting Copyright Registration Proofreading Set up Amazon Account Upload eBooks to Amazon Upload Paperback to Amazon Advertise on LDP's Amazon and Facebook Page

***

Other services available upon request.
Additional charges may apply

Lock Down Publications
P.O. Box 944
Stockbridge, GA 30281-9998
Phone: 470 303-9761
Email: lockdownpublications@gmail.com

Submission Guideline

Submit the first three chapters of your completed manuscript to ldpsubmissions@gmail.com. In the subject line add **Your Book's Title**. The manuscript must be in a Word Doc file and sent as an attachment. Document should be in Times New Roman, double spaced, and in size 12 font. Also, provide your synopsis and full contact information. If sending multiple submissions, they must each be in a separate email.

Have a story but no way to send it electronically? You can still submit to LDP/Ca$h Presents. Send in the first three chapters, written or typed, of your completed manuscript to:

LDP: Submissions Dept
P.O. Box 944
Stockbridge, GA 30281-9998

DO NOT send original manuscript. Must be a duplicate.
Provide your synopsis and a cover letter containing your full contact information.

Thanks for considering LDP and Ca$h Presents.

NEW RELEASES

BLOODLINE OF A SAVAGE 1-3
THESE VICIOUS STREETS 1-3
RELENTLESS GOON 1-3
BY PRINCE A. TAUHID

THE BUTTERFLY MAFIA 1-3
BY FUMIYA PAYNE

A THUG'S STREET PRINCESS 1&2
BY MEESHA

CITY OF SMOKE 3
BY MOLOTTI

GET IT IN SLUGS 1 &2
BY B. STALL

STANDING ON HER BUSINESS 1&2
BY DG SANTANA

STEPPERS 1,2&3
THE REAL BADDIES OF CHI-RAQ
BY KING RIO

THE LANE 1&2
BY KEN-KEN SPENCE

THUG OF SPADES 1&2
LOVE IN THE TRENCHES 2
CORNER BOYS
BY COREY ROBINSON

TIL DEATH 3
BY ARYANNA

THE MURDER QUEENS 8 | MICHAEL GALLON

THE BIRTH OF A GANGSTER 4
BY DELMONT PLAYER

PRODUCT OF THE STREETS 1-3
BY DEMOND "MONEY" ANDERSON

NO TIME FOR ERROR
BY KEESE

MONEY HUNGRY DEMONS 1-2
BY TRANAY ADAMS

HUB CITY MENACE 1-3
BY J. WHITE

A THUGGISH PASSION 1&2
LAND OF DA HOOLIGANZ 1-4
KILLAZ ON STANDBY 1&2
BY IRA B.

FO'EVA ROLLIN 1&2
BY ASSA RAYMOND BAKER

THE LEVEL UP 1&3
BY LUXURY KING

Coming Soon from Lock Down Publications/Ca$h Presents

IF YOU CROSS ME ONCE 6
ANGEL V
By Anthony Fields

A THUGS STREET PRINCESS 3
By Meesha

CORNER BOYS 2
By Corey Robinson

THA TAKEOVER
By Keith Chandler

BETRAYAL OF A G 2
By Ray Vinci

SAVAGE FAMILY EMPIRE 1&2
SOULLESS GOON 1,2&3
THE DIRTY SIDE OF MONEY 1,2&3
By Prince

FOR MY ENEMY'S SAKE
AMBITIONS OF A SLIDER
FRESH OFF DA PORCH
By IRA B.

BY THE TRUCKLOAD 1-4
TIPPIN' THE SCALES 1-3
BAD BITCHES WIT GUNZ 3
PROBLEM SOLVED 2
By Christopher "Diesel" Hornezes

Available Now

RESTRAINING ORDER 1 & 2
By **CA$H & Coffee**

LOVE KNOWS NO BOUNDARIES 1-3
By **Coffee**

RAISED AS A GOON I, II, III & IV
BRED BY THE SLUMS I, II, III
BLAST FOR ME I & II
ROTTEN TO THE CORE I II III
A BRONX TALE I, II, III
DUFFLE BAG CARTEL I II III IV V VI
HEARTLESS GOON I II III IV V
A SAVAGE DOPEBOY I II
DRUG LORDS I II III
CUTTHROAT MAFIA I II
KING OF THE TRENCHES
By **Ghost**

LAY IT DOWN I & II
LAST OF A DYING BREED I II
BLOOD STAINS OF A SHOTTA I & II III
By **Jamaica**

LOYAL TO THE GAME I II III
LIFE OF SIN I, II III
By **TJ & Jelissa**

IF LOVING HIM IS WRONG…I & II
LOVE ME EVEN WHEN IT HURTS I II III
By **Jelissa**

PUSH IT TO THE LIMIT
By **Bre' Hayes**

BLOODY COMMAS I & II
SKI MASK CARTEL I, II & III
KING OF NEW YORK I II, III IV V
RISE TO POWER I II III
COKE KINGS I II III IV V
BORN HEARTLESS I II III IV
KING OF THE TRAP I II
By **T.J. Edwards**

WHEN THE STREETS CLAP BACK I & II III
THE HEART OF A SAVAGE I II III IV
MONEY MAFIA I II
LOYAL TO THE SOIL I II III
By **Jibril Williams**

A DISTINGUISHED THUG STOLE MY HEART I II & III
LOVE SHOULDN'T HURT I II III IV
RENEGADE BOYS 1-4
PAID IN KARMA 1-3
SAVAGE STORMS 1-3
AN UNFORESEEN LOVE 1-3
BABY, I'M WINTERTIME COLD 1-3
A THUG'S STREET PRINCESS 1&2
By **Meesha**

A GANGSTER'S CODE 1-3
A GANGSTER'S SYN 1-3
THE SAVAGE LIFE 1-3
CHAINED TO THE STREETS 1-3
BLOOD ON THE MONEY 1-3
A GANGSTA'S PAIN 1-3
BEAUTIFUL LIES AND UGLY TRUTHS
CHURCH IN THESE STREETS
By **J-Blunt**

CUM FOR ME 1-8
An LDP Erotica Collaboration

THE MURDER QUEENS 8 | MICHAEL GALLON

BLOOD OF A BOSS 1-5
SHADOWS OF THE GAME
TRAP BASTARD
By **Askari**

THE STREETS BLEED MURDER 1-3
THE HEART OF A GANGSTA 1-3
By **Jerry Jackson**

WHEN A GOOD GIRL GOES BAD
By **Adrienne**

THE COST OF LOYALTY 1-3
By **Kweli**

BRIDE OF A HUSTLA 1-3
THE FETTI GIRLS 1-3
CORRUPTED BY A GANGSTA 1-4
BLINDED BY HIS LOVE
THE PRICE YOU PAY FOR LOVE 1-3
DOPE GIRL MAGIC 1-3
By **Destiny Skai**

A KINGPIN'S AMBITION
A KINGPIN'S AMBITION II
I MURDER FOR THE DOUGH
By **Ambitious**

TRUE SAVAGE 1-7
DOPE BOY MAGIC 1-3
MIDNIGHT CARTEL 1-3
CITY OF KINGZ 1&2
NIGHTMARE ON SILENT AVE
THE PLUG OF LIL MEXICO 1&2
CLASSIC CITY
By **Chris Green**

A GANGSTER'S REVENGE 1-4
THE BOSS MAN'S DAUGHTERS 1-5
A SAVAGE LOVE 1&2
BAE BELONGS TO ME 1&2
A HUSTLER'S DECEIT 1-3
WHAT BAD BITCHES DO 1-3
SOUL OF A MONSTER 1-3
KILL ZONE
A DOPE BOY'S QUEEN 1-3
TIL DEATH 1-3
IMMA DIE BOUT MINE 1-6
DYING FOR LIKES
By **Aryanna**

A DOPEBOY'S PRAYER
By **Eddie "Wolf" Lee**

THE KING CARTEL 1-3
By **Frank Gresham**

THESE NIGGAS AIN'T LOYAL 1-3
By **Nikki Tee**

GANGSTA SHYT 1-3
By **CATO**

THE ULTIMATE BETRAYAL
By **Phoenix**

BOSS'N UP 1-3
By **Royal Nicole**

I LOVE YOU TO DEATH
By **Destiny J**

I RIDE FOR MY HITTA
I STILL RIDE FOR MY HITTA
By **Misty Holt**

LOVE & CHASIN' PAPER
By **Qay Crockett**

TO DIE IN VAIN
SINS OF A HUSTLA
By **ASAD**

BROOKLYN HUSTLAZ
By **Boogsy Morina**

BROOKLYN ON LOCK 1 & 2
By **Sonovia**

GANGSTA CITY
By **Teddy Duke**

A DRUG KING AND HIS DIAMOND 1-3
A DOPEMAN'S RICHES
HER MAN, MINE'S TOO 1&2
CASH MONEY HO'S
THE WIFEY I USED TO BE 1&2
PRETTY GIRLS DO NASTY THINGS
By **Nicole Goosby**

LIPSTICK KILLAH 1-3
CRIME OF PASSION 1-3
FRIEND OR FOE 1-3
By **Mimi**

TRAPHOUSE KING 1-3
KINGPIN KILLAZ 1-3
STREET KINGS 1&2
PAID IN BLOOD 1&2
CARTEL KILLAZ 1-3
DOPE GODS 1&2
By **Hood Rich**

THE STREETS ARE CALLING
By **Duquie Wilson**

STEADY MOBBN' 1-3
THE STREETS STAINED MY SOUL 1-3
By **Marcellus Allen**

WHO SHOT YA 1-3
SON OF A DOPE FIEND 1-4
HEAVEN GOT A GHETTO 1&2
SKI MASK MONEY 1&2
By **Renta**

GORILLAZ IN THE BAY 1-4
TEARS OF A GANGSTA 1/&2
3X KRAZY 1&2
STRAIGHT BEAST MODE 1&2
By **DE'KARI**

TRIGGADALE 1-3
MURDA WAS THE CASE 1-3
By **Elijah R. Freeman**

SLAUGHTER GANG 1-3
RUTHLESS HEART 1-3
By **Willie Slaughter**

GOD BLESS THE TRAPPERS 1-3
THESE SCANDALOUS STREETS 1-3
FEAR MY GANGSTA 1-5
THESE STREETS DON'T LOVE NOBODY 1-2
BURY ME A G 1-5
A GANGSTA'S EMPIRE 1-4
THE DOPEMAN'S BODYGAURD 1&2
THE REALEST KILLAZ 1-3
THE LAST OF THE OGS 1-3
By **Tranay Adams**

MARRIED TO A BOSS 1-3
By **Destiny Skai & Chris Green**

KINGZ OF THE GAME 1-7
CRIME BOSS 1-4
By **Playa Ray**

FUK SHYT
By **Blakk Diamond**

DON'T F#CK WITH MY HEART 1&2
By **Linnea**

ADDICTED TO THE DRAMA 1-3
IN THE ARM OF HIS BOSS
By **Jamila**

LOYALTY AIN'T PROMISED 1&2
By **Keith Williams**

YAYO 1-4
A SHOOTER'S AMBITION 1&2
BRED IN THE GAME
By **S. Allen**

TRAP GOD 1-3
RICH $AVAGE 1-3
MONEY IN THE GRAVE 1-3
CARTEL MONEY 1&2
By **Martell Troublesome Bolden**

FOREVER GANGSTA 1&2
GLOCKS ON SATIN SHEETS 1&2
By **Adrian Dulan**

TOE TAGZ 1-4
LEVELS TO THIS SHYT 1&2
IT'S JUST ME AND YOU
By **Ah'Million**

KINGPIN DREAMS 1-3
RAN OFF ON DA PLUG
By **Paper Boi Rari**

THE STREETS MADE ME 1-3
By **Larry D. Wright**

CONFESSIONS OF A GANGSTA 1-4
CONFESSIONS OF A JACKBOY 1-3
CONFESSIONS OF A HITMAN
CONFESSIONS OF A DOPE BOY
By **Nicholas Lock**

I'M NOTHING WITHOUT HIS LOVE
SINS OF A THUG
TO THE THUG I LOVED BEFORE
A GANGSTA SAVED XMAS
IN A HUSTLER I TRUST
By **Monet Dragun**

QUIET MONEY 1-3
THUG LIFE 1-3
EXTENDED CLIP 1&2
A GANGSTA'S PARADISE
By **Trai'Quan**

CAUGHT UP IN THE LIFE 1-3
THE STREETS NEVER LET GO 1-3
By **Robert Baptiste**

NEW TO THE GAME 1-3
MONEY, MURDER & MEMORIES 1-3
By **Malik D. Rice**

CREAM 2-3
THE STREETS WILL TALK
By **Yolanda Moore**

THE STREETS WILL NEVER CLOSE 1-3
By **K'ajji**

LIFE OF A SAVAGE 1-4
A GANGSTA'S QUR'AN 1-4
MURDA SEASON 1-3
GANGLAND CARTEL 1-3
CHI'RAQ GANGSTAS 1-4
KILLERS ON ELM STREET 1-3
JACK BOYZ N DA BRONX 1-3
A DOPEBOY'S DREAM 1-3
JACK BOYS VS DOPE BOYS 1-3
COKE GIRLZ
COKE BOYS
SOSA GANG 1&2
BRONX SAVAGES
BODYMORE KINGPINS
BLOOD OF A GOON
By **Romell Tukes**

CONCRETE KILLA 1-3
VICIOUS LOYALTY 1-3
BLOODY MONEY BAGS
By **Kingpen**

THE ULTIMATE SACRIFICE 1-6
KHADIFI
IF YOU CROSS ME ONCE 1-3
ANGEL 1-4
IN THE BLINK OF AN EYE
By **Anthony Fields**

THE LIFE OF A HOOD STAR
By **Ca$h & Rashia Wilson**

NIGHTMARES OF A HUSTLA 1-3
BLOOD AND GAMES 1&2
By **King Dream**

GHOST MOB
By **Stilloan Robinson**

HARD AND RUTHLESS 1&2
MOB TOWN 251
THE BILLIONAIRE BENTLEYS 1-3
REAL G'S MOVE IN SILENCE
By **Von Diesel**

MOB TIES 1-7
SOUL OF A HUSTLER, HEART OF A KILLER 1-3
GORILLAZ IN THE TRENCHES
OOPS CRY TOO 1&2
THE DAUGHTER OF A CARTEL BOSS
By **SayNoMore**

BODYMORE MURDERLAND 1-3
THE BIRTH OF A GANGSTER 1-4
By **Delmont Player**

FOR THE LOVE OF A BOSS 1&2
By **C. D. Blue**

KILLA KOUNTY 1-5
TENDER
By **Khufu**

MOBBED UP 1-4
THE BRICK MAN 1-5
THE COCAINE PRINCESS 1-10
STEPPERS 1-3
SUPER GREMLIN 1-4
A GANGSTA'S SON
By **King Rio**

MONEY GAME 1&2
By **Smoove Dolla**

A GANGSTA'S KARMA 1-5
By **FLAME**

KING OF THE TRENCHES 1-3
By **GHOST & TRANAY ADAMS**

BAD BITCHES WIT GUNZ 1&2
PROBLEM SOLVED
By "Christopher Diesel" Hornezes

QUEEN OF THE ZOO 1&2
By **Black Migo**

GRIMEY WAYS 1-3
BETRAYAL OF A G
By **Ray Vinci**

XMAS WITH AN ATL SHOOTER
By **Ca$h & Destiny Skai**

KING KILLA 1&2
By **Vincent "Vitto" Holloway**

BETRAYAL OF A THUG 1&2
By **Fre$h**

COUNTDOWN OF A KILLA 1&2
SEX, MURDER AND GOD 1&2
GUNS DOWN, BOTTOMS UP 1&2
By Lo-Life

THE MURDER QUEENS 1-7
By **Michael Gallon**

FOR THE LOVE OF BLOOD 1-4
By **Jamel Mitchell**

HOOD CONSIGLIERE 1&2
NO TIME FOR ERROR
By **Keese**

PROTÉGÉ OF A LEGEND 1,2&3
LOVE IN THE TRENCHES 1&2
By **Corey Robinson**

THE PLUG'S RUTHLESS DAUGHTER 1&2
By **Tony Daniels**

BORN IN THE GRAVE 1-3
CRIME PAYS
By **Self Made Tay**

MOAN IN MY MOUTH
By **XTASY**

TORN BETWEEN A GANGSTER AND A GENTLEMAN
By **J-BLUNT & Miss Kim**

LOYALTY IS EVERYTHING 1-3
CITY OF SMOKE 1-3
By **Molotti**

HERE TODAY GONE TOMORROW 1&2
By **Fly Rock**

WOMEN LIE MEN LIE 1-4
FIFTY SHADES OF SNOW 1-3
STACK BEFORE YOU SPLURGE
GIRLS FALL LIKE DOMINOES
NAÏVE TO THE STREETS
By **ROY MILLIGAN**

PILLOW PRINCESS
By **S. Hawkins**

THE BUTTERFLY MAFIA 1-3
SALUTE MY SAVAGERY 1&2
By **Fumiya Payne**

THE LANE 1&2
By Ken-Ken Spence

THE PUSSY TRAP 1-5
By **Nene Capri**

DIRTY DNA
By **Blaque**

SANCTIFIED AND HORNY
by **XTASY**

BOOKS BY LDP'S CEO, CA$H

TRUST IN NO MAN
TRUST IN NO MAN 2
TRUST IN NO MAN 3
BONDED BY BLOOD
SHORTY GOT A THUG
THUGS CRY
THUGS CRY 2
THUGS CRY 3
TRUST NO BITCH
TRUST NO BITCH 2
TRUST NO BITCH 3
TIL MY CASKET DROPS
RESTRAINING ORDER
RESTRAINING ORDER 2
IN LOVE WITH A CONVICT
LIFE OF A HOOD STAR
XMAS WITH AN ATL SHOOTER